Thelma,
Hope you enjoy enjoyed
the book. Have en_____
you in Church. Hop__
Like Romances.

Joannie

Gold in the Sunshine

By Jean Cowden

Thelma Conner
3595 S 1600 E
Wendell, ID 83355

Gold in the Sunshine

Copyright © 2014 by Jean Cowden

All rights reserved. No part of this book may be used or
reproduced in any manner whatsoever without written
permission except in the case of brief quotations
embodied in critical articles or reviews. For information
address J&J publishing, Box 228, Buhl, Id 83316

ISBN:13:978-1497459540
ISBN:10:1497459540

I dedicate this book to my husband, Jim Cowden, whom I lost in 2001. He stood beside me in everything I did. He was my strongest supporter and my best friend. I still miss you babe.

And my family; my son Cody, daughter Angie, Daughter-in-law Jenny and my sweet little grandson, Michael James.

They gave me the encouragement and help that made everything come together.

J&J Publishing

PO Box # 228

Buhl, Idaho 83316

cow_belle44@hotmail.com

I want to thank Cathy Wilson for all the information she gave me on St. Joseph, her childhood hometown. Also the Blacksnake Hills historical Association for sharing their clippings, pictures and documents.

Most certainly my writer's group, Cathy, Vaughn, Lloyd, Bill, and Marge. They walked me through each chapter.

A special thanks to Cathy for the hours she spent editing it. You guys are priceless!

The picture on the cover is a café and bar in Jarbidge, Nevada, an old mining town just over the southern border of Idaho. This place is still open and serving the public today.

Notice that it didn't take my characters long to get to Jefferson Barracks from St. Joseph. It is actually over 300 miles away, and would have taken about a month. I took a little creative license because I wanted to include it in my story.

Chapter 1
1859

Rumor said he was a hard man, and he knew it was true. He didn't have much use for people, most were never as good as they thought they were. He had known too many liars, fakes, and those who excused themselves for their behavior. He met very few people who were honest and real. The same went for women, and he dealt with them the same way. Most were even worse than men. Fast women at least didn't pretend, scheme, and lie. There wasn't much doubt what they were after.

But he noticed her. She was the new pastor's daughter. He didn't know what it was about her. She was pretty enough, with her sea blue eyes that were so open and expressive and hair that was too dark to be called blonde and too light to be called brown. Watching her from his place as she walked up the boardwalk, he noticed how she greeted everyone with the same open and ready smile. He couldn't believe that she made no distinction between the poor and the well-to-do, the old and the young. In fact she seemed to favor the latter. She had only been in town about a month. Jonah didn't pay attention to preachers and such, but he met the man when he walked into his place. He needed some new shoes put on his mare and a place to keep her. That's what Jonah's business was all about. He had a livery stable and was also the town blacksmith. He traded, sold, rented and boarded horses. Pastor Isaiah Markley was a step above most of his kind. He talked about Sunny. Jonah thought he was talking about his horse until he explained that it was his daughter. Her real name was Sarah, but he had called her sunshine since she was small and the nickname Sunny stuck. When he first saw her, he knew why she caught his eye. She seemed to love life.

It intrigued Jonah, since he was more from the dark and sober side. He never found much joy in life. His Indian mother ran away when he was small, and his dad treated him like the dog he kicked around. When he was about fourteen he struck out on his own and worked every kind of

1

job imaginable. In his late teens he learned the blacksmith trade. He came to St. Jo, a hub for people going west and who needed his service to get there. Jonah had been here for thirteen years and had seen the town grow.

When he first arrived at the age of nineteen in 1846, there had been only about eight-hundred people. Wagon trains came through, but in the spring of '49, when the gold rush started, the streets were lined with prairie schooners, ox carts and anything else that would take them west. The riverboats brought people in by the numbers, and the ferries going across the Missouri were taking them out. The town's population more than doubled. There weren't enough hours in the day to do all the work that people needed done. They paid three and four times the going rate. His business became more and more successful. He couldn't believe the population now in '59. It had tripled. Houses and businesses mushroomed over the last ten years.

At thirty-two he made a decent amount of money, but few people knew that. He didn't need much, so he didn't spend a lot. Jonah bought nice horses, but those turned a profit for him. His place took up a section at the end of town, and the road into St. Jo came right beside his business. His stable housed his blacksmith shop on one side and had an acre of pasture for the horses to roam. He had a small house in the woods just up the road, close enough to keep an eye on his place. It wasn't very big, but it fit his needs. Jonah didn't have any vices, since he saw his alcoholic father die with a wish for a drink on his lips; he knew such things could capture a man. He had a whisky at the saloon every now and then, but never more than a couple. He didn't smoke or chew. Women didn't steal his heart. He did like to read, just about anything. He learned many things through his books, which helped him, since he didn't have much schooling. He improved his skills in the three R's, plus some knowledge in geography, history and things in general.

Missouri had become a slave state in 1820, the first one beyond the Mississippi river. Their neighbors in Kansas hated slavery and there were often fights between them over the issue. Since '54, there had been border wars going on between those who believed in keeping slaves and those who didn't. Many people thought slavery would end, but it became apparent that there would be trouble over the issue. The country was divided, especially along the Missouri and Kansas border.

One day Jonah stepped in when a man was beating a young black boy. He made a deal with the man that if he beat him in a fistfight he would buy the lad from him for the going rate. Jonah won the fight and for fifty dollars acquired young Simon. He hired him and paid him to help do work around his place. He told the boy if he ever wanted to leave he could, that he would personally take him across the border. Simon chose to stay, and he had been with him for eight years.

Jonah watched Sunny as he leaned against the barn door. She knelt down by a little girl and was talking to her. He didn't notice the small girl, but he watched Sunny's face with a full smiling mouth and her sparkling blue eyes. When the mother came out, Sunny talked to her for a minute and then hugged the girl. She waved bye to them, and still smiling she went inside the Blacksnake Trading Post, which had been there since 1821. It was the original St. Joseph, Missouri, founded by Joseph Robidoux.

Jonah pushed away from the door and went back inside. He needed to take care of the horses and get a buggy ready for Mack Reeves, for on Saturday night he went to court Miss Molly Allred. Jonah chuckled. If he didn't stop watching Miss Sunny, he would become as obsessed as Mack was. That wasn't in his character. He was just blood and bones. He wasn't born with the kind of emotion that most people had. He sometimes felt anger for someone if they weren't treated right, and might even step in and give them a hand, but he never had any great emotional strings since he was a kid. Yeah, he was a hard man, he supposed. It wasn't natural for most people to be that way, but for him, that's just the way he was.

"Got my buggy ready, Jonah?" Mack said.

"Sure do. Wouldn't want you to be late to dinner at Miss Molly's."

"You wouldn't believe how sweet that little lady is. Seeing her is the best part of my week. I am going to make her my wife as soon as I get my house built. It's hard to work on it when I'm building so many other places too."

"Business is booming, especially with the railroad finished. I see you're building a hotel now."

"Money makes money, don't it? People like you and me have to swing hammers to make a living. I'd better be on my way. Thanks Jonah."

Jonah tipped his head to acknowledge him as he drove around his place and out of town.

Jonah went to look for Simon and found him locking the last horse in the stall.

"You about to finish everything for the night?" he asked as he laid a hand on his shoulder.

"Sure am Jonah. I just brought in Warrior. He won't come in until all the others are put up."

"He thinks he is the big stallion around here." Jonah said as he slapped his shoulder affectionately. "Okay lock the doors behind you."

"I always do, don't I?" Simon said, grinning.

"Yes, Simon. You're a reliable kid. I'll be home in a little while."

Jonah headed across the street to drop by and see Clay Myers. He was the sheriff and if Jonah had a friend, it was Clay. They were so much alike. They didn't talk much and seemed to have the same ideas. Clay was married and had a couple of kids. He had a dry sense of humor, a ready smile, and like Sunny, seemed to enjoy the things in his life. He was a tough person if the need arose. In his business that happened a lot. Jonah knew that his close friendship with Clay gave him a little more advantage as a half-breed. Between Clay, Joseph, and Mack, he had more backing than most people in his shoes.

"I wondered if you were here or out rounding up the bad guys," Jonah said, as he took a place in a nearby chair.

"If we thought the ferryboats and stagecoaches brought people in, it was nothing compared to the railroad. They have come out of the woodworks."

"I've noticed. I see new faces every day. Do they stay or are they passing through?" Jonah asked.

"A little of both, but most are going west." Clay replied.

"I heard you had a little problem with some border ruffians again."

"I thought all this difference between the Northern and Southern sympathizers would die out, but it's getting worse. The Army usually takes care of those unless they get right up and in my face. A lot of them are young hotheads. We're sure to end up with a war yet. There's a lot of unrest in this nation right now," Clay stated, shaking his head.

"How's that young deputy of yours working out? Is he any help?"

"Not right now. He's lovesick. He's got it bad and can't remember to scratch," Clay answered, shaking his head and smiling with mirth.

"Who has his tail tied in a knot?"

"That new preacher's daughter, Miss Sarah Markley."

"Really, she's barely hit town. I didn't think she had enough time to check the men out yet." Jonah said, barely holding back a cynical tone.

"Oh, it's not her. She doesn't notice him anymore than anybody else. She doesn't seem the least interested, but he keeps sniffing around after her every time he sees her. I don't even mind that, but the rest of the day is spent looking for her. He's scared to death he will miss her somewhere. He's been worthless and can't even remember to pick up the mail," Clay said, chuckling.

"What about Maggie Lou? Isn't she still eyeing the young deputy?"

"My daughter is too young to start that. She's only thirteen. Young Hayden Wells is pushing twenty five."

"Women get married by the time they're fifteen or sixteen," he replied as Clay frowned.

Clay had two young daughters and was a very protective father. They were both cute as could be, and Clay would have his work cut out for him in a few years.

"What'd you think of the preacher's daughter?" Jonah asked, trying to show little interest.

"What'd you think of the preacher's daughter?" Clay said, smiling at Jonah with his eyes twinkling.

"Me! Why should I have an opinion?" he inquired, scowling at his friend.

"I saw you checking her out."

"You're seeing things, old man. Maybe you ought to keep a watch on Maggie Lou instead of everybody else," he stated as he lifted his hat with exasperation and slapped it against his knee.

Clay laughed out loud. "Buddy, you've a right. You're young and single. Marie has been trying to get you interested in a woman for years."

"Your wife is a lovely lady, but I'm not the marrying kind. Tell her not to waste her time."

"Miss Sunny is a fine young woman. Pastor and Mrs. Markley are real nice folks. I think we're lucky to have those kinds of citizens."

"If you say so, I'll take your word for it." Jonah replied, as he replaced his hat and got up. "I'll see ya later."

Clay got up and went to the window and watched Jonah walk down the road headed for his house. Jonah was about a dozen years younger than he was, but he had seemed old from the time he was nineteen, when he first came to St. Joe. He probably told Clay more about his life than anyone, and that wasn't much. He was a private man, but he knew he hadn't had an easy life. He deserved a good woman and some happiness.

Jonah had deep reasons for believing he didn't feel like other people, but Clay thought maybe he had never been loved by anyone and didn't know how it could feel. He wished his friend could find what was lacking in his life. He thought he was one of the best men he had ever known. Marie was probably right, that a good woman could thaw the man out. Clay also knew that people in these parts would never let this good man forget where he came from. He lived in a white man's world all his life, but the color of his skin would always dictate it.

♥

Chapter 2

Sunny saw the blacksmith watching her when she went into the trading post. It wasn't the first time she noticed him. She saw him cross the street when she posted a letter. He was tall and lean with broad shoulders. He had dark hair, almost black. He looked to be of Indian heritage, with dark skin. She asked the lady in the post office about him and she said, "Oh Honey, you don't want to get acquainted with him. He's a tough man and isn't friendly. He doesn't like people. Once he beat a man half to death and took his slave boy. He threw some money at his feet and left him bleeding on the street. Besides," she said, lowering her voice to a whisper. "He's a half-breed."

Sunny did think he looked a little mean, but she hadn't thought he was like that. Her father taught her years ago not to take gossip as fact, to wait to make a judgment call. She decided she would wait and see.

As she walked up the street, she noticed, not for the first time, how many buildings were going up. With the new railroad many people were coming to Saint Jo. The town was accessible to the river, and much of the west was supplied from here. The new hotel was quite impressive, and many people were stopping there. Sunny and her parents had come from a small town in Virginia. She had lived in several places. Her dad believed when the Lord told him to move on, there was a reason for it. She had an older brother still in Virginia with his family. She missed them, but she had always been able to keep her chin up, and make friends. Sunny waved to a couple of ladies talking on the boardwalk, as she turned down the street toward the church.

Joseph Robidoux started the town of St. Jo. He designed the streets and named the main ones after his children. It was the main part of town. She lived down Francis Street, one of many named for them. She was pleased with the location of their house. The street was lined with elm and locust trees. They shaded the house during the humid summer months. The area was full of forest, hills and valleys. There weren't many places that were level and straight. She liked it here. It reminded her of her beloved Virginia.

Some of their neighbors were people who had intended on going west, and had only made it this far. Some broke down and did not have enough money to go farther. A widow now took in laundry and sewing to support her children. Some had been here longer, but they all seemed pleasant enough, if the slavery issue wasn't brought up. The town seemed to be divided on the subject. Her father told her that this issue wasn't going to be solved easily and they all needed to stay in prayer about it. She walked into the house and found her mother in the kitchen, which was her most frequented room. Bess Markley was still attractive for her age, and her family was her highest priority. Sunny had been raised with pure love.

"Hi, Mom. What are you up to?"

"Making a pie. You know how your dad loves sweets."

"It amazes me how many goodies he can put away and still stay slender."

"He's always busy. Sometimes he forgets to eat at all, so he makes up for it when he does."

"Did you bake me some cinnamon crust strips," she asked as she looked around to see. Sunny loved the scraps from the piecrusts, baked with cinnamon and sugar on them. She thought they were better than cookies.

"They are in the oven and should be done by now," she said as she took a towel, opened the oven door and removed them. The smell of cinnamon floated through the room. Her mother's kitchen always smelled so wonderful, with all the great things she cooked. She taught Sunny, and she was a fair hand at it herself. She took a hot piece from the pan, blew on it and took a bite.

"Yummy" she exclaimed, as she chewed a piece.

"I don't think you'll ever outgrow those, will you?" Bess asked, looking at her daughter affectionately as she wiped her hands on her apron.

"Never Mom. In fact, I don't think I'll ever grow up."

"Too late for that. You're a very grown up young lady."

"Spinster you mean. I am already on the shelf at the ripe old age of twenty-three."

"Pooh," Bess said waving her hand. "You are just waiting for the right man. There is nothing wrong with that. I was almost twenty-one when I married your father, and all of my friends had been married for a few years. I have never been sorry that I took my time. Love is worth the wait."

Sunny always had plenty of beaus, but she just had never felt that something special in her heart. The deputy was flirting with her, but she didn't feel any real attraction.

♥

Chapter 3

Sunny often went with her father to call on his parishioners. She hadn't gone outside of town yet, so she decided to accompany him today. He would need his buggy, so they walked toward Alexander's stables, where they boarded their mare and rig. A young black boy met them at the door.

"Hi, Simon, I hope you're having a fine day. Young man, do you think you could ready my horse and buggy?" Isaiah asked, placing his hand on his daughter's arm, "This is my daughter, Sarah, but we call her Sunny."

Sunny took his hand and shook it, smiling at him. "Hi Simon, I'm glad to meet you. Do you work here?"

"Yes, Ma'am," he replied as he dropped his hand from hers.

"Don't call me Ma'am, call me Sunny, okay?"

Simon nodded his head, "I will go hook your buggy up." he answered, as he turned into the building. Sunny looked up just as Jonah came toward them. He was even better looking up close, but he did look like a tough man. Her father greeted him with a friendly smile.

"Hi, Jonah. How are you today?"

"I'm fine, how are you, Pastor?"

"Call me Isaiah. This is my daughter, Sunny. Dear, this is Jonah Alexander."

"How do you do, Mr. Alexander," she said as she looked at him a little uncertain.

Jonah tipped his hat at her. "Glad to meet you, Ma'am. Is Simon getting your rig?" he asked, as he turned his eyes toward her father.

"Yes, he is. He was right on the ball. That's a nice young helper you have there."

Jonah didn't answer as Simon came out with the buggy. He bounded from it, handing the reins to Isaiah. Sunny started toward the buggy and Jonah took her arm, supporting her while she climbed in.

"Thank you," she said as she settled into the seat.

"You're welcome. Have a nice ride," he replied, touching his hat again. Sunny smiled at him as her father pulled the buggy into the street. While they rode along she watched the beautiful countryside as her father pointed out some landmarks but Sunny barely took in his words. Her mind was on Jonah Alexander. What was it about the man? He looked almost mean, but she thought there was something deeper in him. He seemed to be a real mystery. Her dad genuinely liked him, but of course he liked most people. Time would tell, but she certainly noticed his intense hazel eyes. His hair was as black as night with shots of red and brown running through it in the sunlight. He looked less like an Indian than she had previously thought, but he sure had the fierce look of one. She thought he was probably more dangerous.

"It's a beautiful place here, Papa. Who would believe that all those border wars have been going on so long? It seems so peaceful," she claimed.

"St. Jo hasn't been touched much by all that, they say. Evidently there is German militia that patrols this area that helps the Union Army. Most of the trouble all takes place farther south"

"Where are we going today?"

"We are going to call on the McCallesters', the Owen's family and Richard Reed. They live several miles from town, and I haven't visited them yet."

"I know the McCallesters'. I remember they were in church the first week we came here. The Owen's come every Sunday, but I don't remember any Richard Reed. Who is he?"

"I haven't met him before, but the people in church tell me he used to come with his wife and teenage sons until she died last year. I thought I would drop by and see him too."

"What do you think of the blacksmith?"

"Jonah's a real no-nonsense kind of man but I think he's one of the good guys. Why?" He asked, as he looked at his daughter.

"A lady in the post office told me he was mean."

"I think Jonah has to put up with a lot of racial feelings."

"Because he's half Indian? When are people going to learn that what race we are has nothing to do with who we are?"

"We hope someday people will be wiser but some still feel those old prejudices. So why are you asking about that particular man?" he asked with a teasing twinkle in his eyes.

"Come on, Papa. I just met him," she replied, wrinkling her nose at him in exasperation. Her father was always trying to figure out who she might be interested in.

Jonah heard her youthful voice talking to Simon. He hadn't been able to help himself. He wanted to see her up close, and he hadn't been disappointed. She had the most genuine smile, and her blue eyes were full of warmth. She didn't seem to have a drop of snobbery in her. Her honey colored hair sparkled in the sunshine underneath her straw bonnet. He was surprised when he helped her into the buggy, for her hands were slightly calloused. That meant she knew what work was all about. She wasn't some pampered, spoiled, girl. Her eyes looked as innocent as a child's, however she was fully-grown. He guessed her past twenty. She seemed to be a little guarded when he helped her into the buggy. He didn't know if she had heard tales about him or was naturally that way with strangers.

"What are you thinking, you fool? A white woman is the last thing you need to be thinking about," he mumbled to himself as he went back to work. Well, he had seen her up close, and that was the end of it. He would forget about her.

*   *

He was wrong, for the very next day Simon had gone to the Trading Post. That was the only place that Jonah allowed him to go alone. He knew Joseph would look out for him if trouble came. Simon always took his dog. Jonah found the puppy when he first came to live with him. He thought it would help him get over his fears. Brat became his pal, and they went everywhere together. Brat did a good job of protecting him.

When he went inside the store the dog always waited outside. When Jonah saw him lying on the porch of the Trading Post he knew Simon was probably after some of his favorite stick candy. Jonah had been in the blacksmith shop, forming some horseshoes. When he finished he walked over and got himself a drink of water. When he drained the dipper and poured some around his neck, he looked up and saw Simon walk out the door with his bag of candy, and right beside him was Sunny. She was talking to Simon as she walked along with him. He watched them start toward his stables with Brat in tow. Sunny turned toward the dog and held her hand slowly out to him. Simon urged him to sniff her hand, which was an introduction for Brat to know that she was a friend. The dog sniffed, and then let her rub his shiny black head. Jonah knew she was now part of the small circle that was allowed to touch the dog. He stood there and watched them continue on, passing the stables toward the pasture. Puzzled, Jonah buttoned his shirt, and decided to go around the building and see what they were doing. He knew he wanted a chance to see her. Why kid himself. She was standing on the railing of the fence, rubbing the nose of Gypsy, a newly acquired sorrel mare. She was telling Simon how beautiful she was, and Gypsy seemed to understand her.

"Hi, you lovely lady," she uttered, while rubbing her head. "How old is she?"

"I don't know Ma'am, Jonah just got her."

"What'll he do with her?"

"I don't know Ma'am, maybe sell her." Simon surmised.

"She's too special to sell, but business is business I guess. Do you ever get attached to any of them?"

"Sometimes" he answered.

"We board Lady here. You know the gray dapple."

"Yes Ma'am, I know. We take good care of them. Jonah, don't let anyone mistreat his animals," Simon declared.

"He looks like he takes good care of you too," she said, smiling at him.

"Yes Ma'am. He took me away from a mean man that beat me. I was only six, and Jonah told me nobody would ever do that to me again."

"Simon, I told you to call me Sunny or Sarah. I hope I'm your friend, and my friends don't call me Ma'am,"

Jonah walked up beside her, and placed his hand on Gypsy's ear.

"You like my new little girl?" he asked, looking at Sunny. She turned and looked at him, and Jonah was shocked for she looked at him like he was her hero. He couldn't take his eyes from her. What had changed since yesterday? He'd thought that she'd been a little unsure of him when he helped her into the buggy.

"Simon told me you rescued him from a mean person when he was six. Jonah you're a good person."

"Don't bet on it. Just ask a lot of people in this town. I am not the most liked person here."

"You let them think those things," she answered smiling sweetly at him. "You're a fraud Mr. Alexander, but I have you figured out."

"Young women with brains don't come near me." he replied, smiling.

She turned back to Gypsy. "You don't seem to be scared, and if you're not, I won't be," she said, speaking to the horse as she looked back over her shoulder at Jonah. He thought maybe he should be the scared one. This lady could be dangerous.

* *

15

Jonah didn't see her up close for awhile, but he saw her across the street most days. The young deputy, Hayden, always seemed to be walking her to or from some place. There was no doubt Jonah was enamored of her. He shook his head, knowing he would get over it. She was just another woman, a dime a dozen. She may be just a little more intriguing which grabbed his attention, but she was white and way out of his reach.

Jonah figured that once she had been around for awhile he would be less fascinated. He hoped so because he seemed to think of her way too often.

As Sunny was leaving the post office one day, she looked across the street and saw Gypsy near the fence. The horse seemed to be looking at her. She was a beautiful animal. She walked over, set her reticule down on the ground, and stepped upon the railing of the fence. Gypsy moved closer and started to nuzzle her. Sunny started rubbing her well-shaped head.

"Good morning, gorgeous," she crooned. "You are so sweet, little girl. Are you looking for company? Me too. We'll just have a little visit, okay? Do you wish you could go for a walk? I would like to ride you, but I don't think Jonah would allow it. I'm not that great at it." Simon stepped from the stables and heard her talking to Gypsy.

"Hello, Simon. I just dropped by to say hello. How are you today?" she asked.

"Fine, Ma'am"

"Can't you talk to me?" she inquired, tipping her head at him and smiling.

"Yes, Ma'am," he replied as he walked closer to the fence.

"I wish I knew how to ride. I would love to ride her."

"Would you really like to ride her?" he asked, as he came closer to the fence.

"Yes I would, but I have only been on a horse a few times. I don't think Jonah would appreciate it if something happened to this special horse."

"Jonah likes the horses exercised. Sometimes I ride them around the corral. He might let you ride her there."

"I would love that, but I don't ride too well."

"I didn't know how to ride when I first came to live with Jonah. He taught me," Simon explained.

"It looks like Jonah taught you a lot." Sunny stated.

"Yes Ma'am. He has taught me to take care of horses and how to blacksmith. He told me when the day came that I wanted to go live in the free states, I would have a trade."

"Do you plan on doing that?"

"When I'm older I might. Jonah says there might be a war soon, and we might all be free, if things go right."

"I think so too. That seems to be what all the unrest is about. Where are your parents, Simon?" she asked tenderly.

"All I know is when I was sold, we lived in South Carolina. Jonah couldn't take me there because I was too young and didn't know where in South Carolina. All I knew was the master was called John. Jonah said he didn't know enough to take me back. When I get older, I will go look for them."

"Do you have brothers and sisters?"

"Yes Ma'am, Jeb was my older brother, and Mamie was my baby sister." Simon answered.

"What is your last name?" Sunny asked.

"I didn't know my last name. Jonah gave me the name Freeman. He says I was a free man the minute he got me, so now my name is Simon Freeman."

Sunny felt a lump in her throat. She could have cried. People talked about Jonah being a hard and unforgiving man, but she knew better. She was admiring him more and more. Everything she'd learned impressed her. Most people bragged about their goodness, but here was a young boy that he did so much for, and everyone called him Jonah's boy. He was more like Jonah's child.

"How old are you, Simon? You are almost as tall as Jonah" Sunny guessed.

"I will be fifteen the first day of May," he replied proudly.

"Less than two weeks. What is your favorite cake?" she asked, grinning with pleasure.

"I like them all. Jonah always has Mrs. Myers bake me one and she sure can bake. I eat most of it myself."

Yes, Simon looked about fifteen. He was a head shorter than Jonah, but had a young boy's build, thin and gangly. His shoulders were beginning to broaden out, probably from swinging the blacksmith hammer and lifting pitchforks of hay. He was almost a man, but still a boy. Every time she looked at Simon, her thoughts were of the man who raised him. This unselfish man took a young boy to raise, not as a slave, but like a son, not asking for anything in return. She didn't think he knew how special he was.

"Hello, Miss Sunny. How are you today?" Deputy Hayden said as he walked up beside her.

"I'm just talking to Simon and admiring Gypsy."

"It is a nice horse. Jonah usually buys good horseflesh," he declared, as he lifted his leg upon the fence railing, brushing against her skirts. Sunny felt him move in closer than was necessary. She moved over, giving him more room.

"I would join you at church on Sundays, but that is my day on duty."

"You're certainly welcome anytime," she stated, as she stepped down from the fence. "I have to get home. It was nice talking to you, Simon," she announced, as she turned and waved at him. Deputy Hayden looked at her wrinkling his brow following beside as she headed for home.

"You shouldn't be so friendly with that black kid. You know that Jonah's a breed don't you?"

"I have no concern where people come from," she declared sharply.

"I don't know what things were like in Virginia, but here we stay in our place."

18

Sunny stopped and turned to him, "What are you trying to tell me deputy? That I'm not allowed to visit with people in Saint Jo unless I know who their parents are? Where were your parents from?"

"Well they sure weren't from some Indian or African village."

"Do you feel like that makes you better?" she replied, exasperated.

"Well sure, God made us all different for a reason."

"And what reason was that?" Sunny could feel herself getting mad.

"Well, different people in different places."

Sunny had enough of his bigoted talk, she turned to him, took a deep breath.

"So as you see it, the lowest tasks go to people with black and dark brown skin, and they should be slaves or at least looked down upon. And those of us that have lily white skin should be the owners or at least have bigger and more important tasks in the world. You do know that Jesus had dark skin don't you?"

"No he didn't."

"Read your Bible, Deputy. He was a Jew. He had dark skin. While you're reading about him, notice the ignorant people who crucified him," she stated sharply as her voice reached a high tone as she ended her comment. She stalked off, leaving the deputy standing in the middle of the sidewalk.

♥

Chapter 4

Sunny stopped by the stables to talk to Simon and Jonah when she was in town. Sometimes she brought Simon cookies, or homemade bread, which delighted him. He never said much, but his eyes would light up and he would politely say, "Thank you, Ma'am."

Jonah couldn't kid himself. He looked forward to her visits too. He'd tried not to go near her, but he was drawn against his will. Simon had the same problem. He didn't have many friends. Most people were kind enough to him, because Jonah wouldn't allow anyone to mistreat him. There were some slave owners in St. Jo, but there were a lot of common people who didn't have any. There were a few young slaves Simon's age, but weren't exactly told they could go hang around with pals. People that Simon was comfortable with were older friends of Jonah. He liked the attention that Sunny gave him, but knew his place and only answered her questions.

*   *

She learned from Simon that his fifteenth birthday was on Wednesday. She asked Jonah if he'd come to her house and bring Simon for supper. He'd told her that some people would not think highly of her for having a black boy as a guest. She didn't care what people thought. She had to live by what she felt was right. He'd told her rumors would start about them, saying that Jonah was courting her. That didn't bother her either. In fact, she asked him with a wicked little smile if he was afraid of that rumor himself. She didn't know how much he'd thought about that. He was smart enough to know he wasn't good enough for her. Sunny was a special woman, and he could never deserve her. She was a little upset with him and called him stubborn when he wouldn't agree to the birthday party. Jonah knew she just didn't know how that would cause more problems than it would be worth.

Jonah walked across the street to Clay's office. He liked to talk to him, but he hadn't been around much in the last few days. He walked in and took a chair and tipped his hat back.

"Haven't seen you much this week, what's going on?"

"I've been busy as a grasshopper in fall. Seems like somethin's been going on everywhere, and when I need Hayden to do some of the small chores, he ain't around. Robidoux's been trying to keep things civil between the Indians and the railroad men. The Indians are riled up over the railroaders shooting the buffalo, and letting them lay and rot out there. They tell us they are a hazard to their train." Clay drawled in his slow, southern Georgia dialect, shaking his head in frustration.

"Well, if anyone can pacify the Indians, Joseph can. He's been fur trading with them for forty years. He's had more pow-wow's with them than anybody I know."

"Even Joseph can't talk to them. How can he explain away what they're doing? He has tried to tell the railroad's bigwigs that the buffalo is their livelihood, right down to the hides. They won't listen; those big shot educated men don't care about anything but money and power. The Union Army always has its hands full with the boarder ruffians, now they have to get into the railroad's problems. What a mess this country is coming to."

"Anything I can do to help?"

"There's not even anything I can do, Jonah. Things are moving over us that we don't like, but we can't stop it. It doesn't look like anything except war is coming. I can't believe we are going to have to fight our own countrymen."

"Are you going to fight, if it comes to that?"

"I'm going to try and take care of this town until the dust clears. Let's hope it won't be too long or too bloody. How about you?"

"It's not my war. I plan on protecting Simon, and the rest can go to blazes."

"What about protecting a young preacher's daughter with big blue eyes and a sunshine of a smile?" Clay said, smiling broadly.

"Where in the world do you dig up these ideas of yours?" Jonah scowled.

"We haven't failed to notice that she stops by and sees you quite often. The young deputy hasn't failed to notice either, and it's eatin' at him. It makes him as useless to me as a three legged dog."

"She's being a friend to Simon. She has sympathy for people in need."

"And what does Simon need. He looks like a well adjusted young man," Clay said, getting a real kick out of Jonah's hard-nosed expression.

"Are you trying to say something here? If you are, you're wrong. I'm a hard man, she's a real lady. She stops by, and Simon and I chat with her. She brings Simon cookies and bread sometimes," he snapped as he jerked his hat lower on his head. Clay laughed out loud. He knew Jonah always jerked on his hat when he was frustrated. He also knew he was denying his statement too adamantly not for there to be some truth to it. He knew his friend well, and he usually didn't even take the time to deny anything anyone thought. He never cared what they said.

"I'm funnin' you old friend. You'll do what you want. Just know that the deputy is jealous. He asks her to go with him several times to different places, and she always tells him no, but he notices that she stops by your place."

"I'm not good enough for her, but neither is the young deputy."

"You plan on picking out somebody for her?"

"No, she'll do a good enough job on her own when the time comes."

"I'm sure she will," Clay surmised.

"She wanted me to bring Simon by her house on his birthday for a surprise birthday supper. She wasn't happy, but I told her no. Some people in this town wouldn't take to the idea too highly. They think it's alright for Simon to intermingle with men, like you and Joseph, but a sit down dinner at someone's table, I just don't think so."

"That would be a nice thing for Simon, but I can see your point. It might cause a lot of problems, especially now with feelings running so high on both sides."

"I noticed some drovers at the bar the other day, making a lot of hoop-de-la. You got a trail drive near?" Jonah asked.

"Yeah, like there isn't enough going on around here? They get paid when they get the cattle to the railhead and stop at every watering hole between there and wherever they call home. Most of them are good boys, but they can get into a lot of trouble when they are downing the hard stuff.

"I saw a couple of them eyeing Sunny one day. I told her to stay on the opposite side of the street from the saloons. She thinks everyone in the world is as nice as she is."

"So you think she's nice, do you?" Clay asked, chuckling.

"Aw hell, Can't talk to you anymore without you making something outta nothin'." Jonah said getting out of his chair and pulling his hat down over his eyes. He walked to the door, then stopped and looked back. "Just to tell you again, I'm not the marryin' kind, besides Clay you know where I come from. That's not the kind of man that she needs. The white part of me that comes from my father is the part that is hard and tough, and won't let anyone push me around. The Indian side of me that comes from my mother keeps me reminded that I can't have what other men do," he said, as he turned and left.

Clay shook his head. Jonah hadn't had an easy life. Being raised by his worthless father, and being half Indian, had left him fighting giants.

He deserved a good woman like Miss Markley, but he knew it could never really happen in these parts, at least not right now. He didn't know anybody who deserved it more than Jonah. Life just wasn't fair.

"Where the blazes have you been?" Clay asked, as young deputy Hayden walked in with a scowl on his face.

"I asked Miss Sunny to go to the church picnic with me, but she told me no. I think she's got a hankerin' for Jonah. I saw him leave here. Did he say anything to you about her?"

"No, what makes you think that?"

"Miss Sunny got mad at me last week when I told her she shouldn't talk so freely to Simon and Jonah. She hasn't been very friendly to me since."

"I can't say as I blame her. Jonah and Simon don't bother anybody. She stops by and talks to them of her own free will. They don't chase her down."

"I know Jonah is your friend, but he is still a breed and a girl like her should mind herself."

"Hayden, you are one narrow minded kid. You just remember he is my friend, my very best friend, and I wouldn't take kindly to any problems you laid at Jonah's door. Do you understand me, or do I have to draw you a map?" Clay commanded, stressing his words seriously.

"Yeah, I understand you Clay," he said, swallowing his true feelings.

♥

Chapter 5

Sunny didn't get to give Simon a birthday dinner, but she brought him a big luscious cake, a homemade card and a hatband that she found at the leather shop.

Simon was pleased and kept talking about it almost up until bedtime. After he fell asleep, Jonah was on the front porch. A breeze was blowing, and the night was full of stars. He wished they had been able to go to a real sit down dinner at Sunny's house, like she suggested, but it just wasn't possible. He remembered dreaming of homey things like that as a child. He sure hadn't come far since those days. He would never be welcome in fine people's houses since he was kept in his place. It had put a big want inside of him. He needed to stay away from her; she made him feel things he didn't want to. She would complicate his life.

He sat down on the railing and watched all the lights fade from the houses in his view. People were blowing out their lanterns and going to bed. Most of those people had families, but Jonah knew that was something he would never have. He didn't know the first thing about families. He had a little experience raising Simon, but he had been a smart child, and came already half trained. He got up and went inside. It was time to go to bed. He would try to think of her as a friend that Simon needed, and maybe he could fool himself into believing that.

*　　*

"She would like to learn to ride, but I think she would like to ride Gypsy. Do you think she can go fishing with us the next time we go," Simon asked Jonah as they let the horses out to pasture.

"Did she ask you to ask me?"

"No, she just said she wished she could ride better, but I thought it might be okay. Jonah knew he should try to stay away from her but it just seemed like everything was working against him, especially his own will.

"I guess she could ride Gypsy around the pasture until I see how she does. As far as going riding with us to Blacksnake hills, I will have to give that some thought."

"'Maybe her papa could come along."

"That's not a bad idea, Simon. I always knew you were a smart kid."

Sunny's riding lessons started in the pasture. After Jonah decided she was doing well enough, he let Simon ride with her up and down the street. She insisted on learning how to saddle and bridle the horse herself. It took a little time to learn how to heave the saddle upon Gypsy's back, but after a few days she accomplished the task.

Simon showed her how to curry the horse after they got back from their ride. It didn't take her long to master that as well. She loved being around the horses and didn't miss many days of riding. People started teasing her about being a real wrangler.

She charmed old and young alike with her infectious smile and joyful laughter. Jonah admired the fact that she called Simon and him her friends. She wasn't the least bit ashamed of them. Most people accepted the fact and didn't seem shocked to see her at the stables. Jonah was glad because he thought he would really miss this woman who had brought such sunshine into their lives. He gave up on staying away from her. He would always welcome the sight of Sunny when she came around, but knew that's all he would ever be able to look forward to.

As she progressed in her riding abilities, Jonah agreed that if her father would come along, they would all ride to Blacksnake creek and fish for a few hours on Sunday.

Sunny was excited about riding to the creek. It was only a few miles away, and better than riding around the pasture and up and down the street in front of the stables.

Sunny and her father followed Jonah and Simon, but somewhere along the way, Sunny ended up beside Jonah following her father and Simon. Sunny noticed that

Jonah had a gun belt on, plus a rifle in the scabbard of the saddle. They rode quietly for a few minutes, making their way through the trees and along a wide trail.

"You're armed pretty heavy," she commented.

"You need to take precautions. Snakes, cougars and even a rogue bear can be about sometimes," he said calmly.

"Or maybe raiding Indians. Maybe a dispute between differences of opinions."

Surprised, Jonah looked at her. "Just being prepared."

"I know what's going on in the world. I don't hide my head in dress patterns, and the latest hat fashions. My parents have never kept things from me."

"I can see that," he replied, settling his hat onto his head.

"It's beautiful up here," she said, looking around at the forest.

"I can't deny that. I've always liked it here," he said, as he watched her straight posture in the saddle. She rode well for a beginner.

"Have you always lived here?" she asked, looking at him.

"No, I grew up in Maryland. I came here when I was young, and opened the blacksmith shop."

"When did you open the stable?"

"In early spring of '48."

"When did you get Simon?" she asked, as she patted Gypsy's neck.

"Eight years ago. He was almost seven," Jonah answered, watching her as she rode along the trail, looking contented.

"Did you teach him to read?" she asked, lifting an eyebrow, and smiling at him.

Again Jonah looked at her in surprise, wondering why she had asked that.

"It's against the law to teach slaves how to read and write. I wondered if you taught him. He read his birthday card the other day," she explained.

"He's free, but legally I own him, for his safety. I taught him and he loves to read. I can't keep enough books around."

"Simon is lucky you rescued him. I shudder to think how he would have spent his life with a man who treated him badly. He wouldn't be the pleasant young man that he is today. You're a good man," she stated, looking at him. He couldn't quite pull his eyes away from hers.

"I'm hard-nosed. Just ask the right people, they will tell you," he replied looking away.

"You're a caring man, and you know it," she answered, smiling. She took a deep breath, and sighed, "Do you think we are going to war, Jonah?"

He shook his head assenting, "It sure is looking that way."

"If we do, I sure hope it's worth the fight for the slaves. Somebody needs to come out of it a victor."

They rode up to a creek and dismounted. Jonah took the saddles from the horses and hobbled them, so they wouldn't wander off. They started eating the tall green grass.

They all threw their lines into the water. Jonah stood with his pole; he didn't want to become too lax. He knew these were tougher times with all the unrest, and didn't want to take any chances of being caught off guard. They really hadn't had much trouble this far north, but he didn't want to get too sure about it. He taught Simon since he was young to listen for noises and keep aware of what was around him. Sunny trusted everybody, and thought the world was a nice place. He wouldn't be surprised if Isaiah didn't feel the same way.

Isaiah and Simon were sitting on the grass beside the river. Sunny found a big flat rock further upstream. Jonah watched her take her hat off and throw in her line. She settled down comfortably. Some of her hair came loose from her stylish bun. The wind picked up the honey colored hair and blew it around.

She thought he was a good man, if she only knew where he came from. He lived in shacks that were ready to fall in and slept on smelly blankets on a cold dirt floor. He scoured garbage pits for food most of his young life.

Jonah barely remembered his mother. She was Indian and the only memories of her were asking him to be good so he wouldn't upset his father. He knew the old man slapped her around. One day she saw an opportunity to leave, so she did, but without him.

Then it was he that got slapped around, until he got big enough to fight back. The old man was so drunk all the time that he could easily knock him down. When his father took his last breath, Jonah felt no remorse. He left with the rags he had on and never looked back.

He worked as a ranch hand doing the lowliest jobs until he learned to rope and ride. He saved his money and bought a horse and saddle. An old gunslinger taught him how to use a gun. He made him practice until he was lightning fast. He gave him some good advice, telling him not to let anyone know how fast he could draw, or all he would be doing is watching his back. Jonah was glad he listened.

A German man taught him to blacksmith, and that made him a good living over the past decade or so. He wondered what Sunny would think of him if she knew about his past. He had done well for himself, but he had never been able to wash the grime of his childhood away.

Everybody caught a few brook trout. Sunny asked if they wanted to join them for supper and she and her mother would fry them up. Jonah immediately came up with an excuse, saying they couldn't. He saddled the horses and they were soon on their way back. When they returned to the stables he helped Sunny from Gypsy. She slid into his arms as he helped her down and she kept her hands on his shoulders after she was on the ground.

"Thank you, Jonah. You took time to teach me to ride, and it was a special day today. I haven't enjoyed myself so much in a long time," she said, looking at him tenderly.

His knees were almost weak from looking into her serious blue eyes. He moved away from her

"You're welcome," he said, hoarsely.

Isaiah shook Jonah's hand and thanked him for a nice day, and then he and his daughter headed for home.

*   *

Jonah let Simon do some blacksmith work. He worked at the forge with ease. He was pleased, for he was getting better all the time. He built arm muscles that looked out of place with his skinny frame. He knew he would grow into himself in a few years.

"Got the kid doing your work?" Clay said, interrupting them.

"He's going to be better than me one of these days. Take a seat." Clay walked to the corner and sat on a nail keg. Jonah poured them a cup of coffee and sat down, handing Clay one.

"Have you heard the news?" Clay asked, as he took the coffee from him.

"You mean about the Pony Express? Yeah that's quite the buzz. Have you read the notice? I have one nailed on the wall." Jonah got up and went over and ripped it down, and returned to his seat.

"It says,

"Wanted. Young, skinny, wiry fellows. Not over 18. Must be expert riders. Willing to risk death daily. Orphans preferred."

This is a new fast way to get mail to California, I understand."

"Yeah, William Russell started the Leavenworth & Pikes Peak Express last year. Then last winter he incorporated it, with a couple of guys named Jones and Smoot. They were running stagecoaches from Leavenworth to Denver. Then by some smooth move they obtained The Hockaday's mail route. They have been running their stagecoaches from here to Salt lake City ever since June."

"So why isn't that good enough. The coaches leave here every day," Jonah said, as he laid the advertisement down.

"Well, I hear they're not doing so good money wise. The creditors are knocking at their door. I hear tell he is asking his old partners Majors and Waddell to go in with him for this new project."

"Still doesn't explain why they'll need riders instead of coaches." Jonah said, wrinkling his brow.

"How long have you had this coffee on? It's thick as mud," Clay said, looking at the cup disgustingly.

"Since early morning. Hey, it makes you tough." Jonah said, laughing.

Well I'm not that tough," Clay said, as he tossed it out and laid his cup on the ground.

"So answer my question, Why riders instead of coaches?"

"The government is going to pay a million dollars for a mail contract." Clay said.

Jonah let out a whistle. "That's quite a hunk of money," he exclaimed, pushing his hat back on his head.

"Yeah, I think they're trying to get public attention, and show how fast they can get the mail to California. They plan on ten days."

"Can they do it?"

"From what I hear, they plan to have lots of riders and horses. They'll get fresh horses every fifteen to twenty miles," Clay said, as he seated himself a bit more comfortably on the keg.

"How far will each one ride?" Jonah said, as he tossed his coffee away too.

"I hear around seventy-five to a hundred miles a day. Coming from the east and west at the same time. They will meet at certain points and will eat and sleep a while before making their return trip"

"It's the age of progress isn't it? And I thought ten years ago when Levi Strauss made these durable pants that we all wear, now that was progress." Both men laughed, for

31

they had talked about that being the greatest invention in years.

"When's all this going to come about?" Jonah asked.

"Who knows? I hear the deals are in the works. Majors and Waddell are going to get their way on this deal because they are the guys with the money. Mack Reeves told me the other day that they wanted him to enlarge and improve the stables. So it sounds like it won't be too far off."

"Well, that's all anybody is talking about today. We will have to watch and see," Jonah said, as he got up and put the coffee cups on a shelf.

"We will see if they pull it off," Clay said, getting up.

I was talking to Mack the other day and he finished his house, so Molly and he are going to tie the knot soon," Jonah commented as he and Clay leaned against the door, looking out into the street.

"Is he the only one?" Clay asked, grinning.

"Don't start that again, or I will throw you right out that door," Jonah said, half smiling himself.

"I heard you went fishing with the blue-eyed beauty on Sunday."

"For your information, her father was invited too."

"That's how you do it; butter up the preacher man to get his daughter."

"If you weren't my friend, I would kick your tail. It's bad enough when Simon is asking me if I'm going to court her."

"The boy just wants a family. Nothin' wrong with that."

Jonah pulled his hat down over his eyes and shook his head. "Ain't going to happen my friend."

"You can't tell me you don't like her. I've never seen you have such a spring in your step, or whistle so much."

"We're just friends. Sunny is friends with everyone. You notice she still lets the young deputy walk her down the street. Don't make up things that aren't there. Even if she was willing, it just wouldn't work and you know it."

"I know." Clay answered shaking his head. He knew that neither he, nor Jonah, had to say the word, half-breed. He knew some things were just not accepted in this country. It was downright awful, for Jonah was a better man than most of the whites he knew.

"She likes my horses," Jonah stated, smiling.

"Yeah, she likes your horses" Clay replied, mischievously. "Well I'd better make a round before quitting time. See you around." He slapped Jonah affectionately on the shoulder and walked over and looked at the door hinges that Simon had just finished making. "That's a good job, Simon. You're going to be a great blacksmith someday," he said, as he patted him on the shoulder. Simon beamed with pride.

♥

Chapter 6

Autumn came to St. Jo, and the trees turned to gold, red and brown. Mack Reeves married Molly Allred in late September. They planned to move into their newly built home on Charles Street. Jonah didn't go to many social functions but Mack asked him to come. The bride was beautiful and Mack had eyes only for his brand new wife. The crowd moved outside behind the church for the reception. Sawhorses and wood planks had been set up with piles of food. Jonah filled his plate and moved over and stood beneath a big oak tree. He couldn't keep his eyes off of Sunny. She was beautiful in a lavender dress that made her eyes more blue and her hair more gold. He tried not to look directly at her, but watched her from the corner of his eyes. She moved through the crowd talking to everyone like a good preacher's daughter. He was eating when she moved over to him.

"Hello Jonah. How are you tonight?" she asked, with a teasing smile.

"It's a sad day to watch a friend fall," he replied, smiling with mischief. Sunny threw back her head and laughed.

"Men act like marriage is a fate worse than death. It's an act. They just make woman feel bad enough to wait on them the rest of their life." Sunny joined in when Jonah laughed.

"You may be right," he admitted.

"I just barely got to know Molly, and I really like her. I am glad she is going to live in town so we might spend a little time together. I only met Mack a couple of times."

"Mack is a good guy. He works hard, minds his own business, and he loves Miss Molly," Jonah said, emphasizing the last few words, with a wink.

"She loves him too." Sunny said, whispering the words back, smiling. "I would say that's a good start for them."

Jonah looked up and saw a couple of people watching them a little too interested. He made an excuse to her, moved away, walked to the table and sat his plate down, wandered over to the newlyweds and shook hands with Mack. After a short conversation, he left. The last person he wanted to hurt was Sunny. He needed to watch out since he had become too lax around her. He enjoyed her company and had forgotten to notice things that could cause a real problem.

*   *

Autumn 1859

Since the railroad arrived, passengers could get where they were going faster and easier. Cattle, raw materials, and other products were shipped by rail. The town gained more people by the day. Strangers stopped off on their way to other places. The new hotel got more and more business. The deal went through that originated the Pony Express. They planned on starting in the spring. The problems between the North and South still existed. John Brown was hanged at Harpers Ferry for inciting an uprising of slaves. Mayor Thompson led a crowd of people to the post office and tore down the American flag and shredded it. The town was split in its politics. St. Joe made a town ordinance that neither Union nor Confederate flag could fly anywhere in town. The discussion was held over using a local flag.

The Indians hated the Iron Horse, and caused problems. On one hand things were good, and on the other, things were bad. Jonah watched the town grow over the years, and even though he had more business than ever, he liked the smaller town.

One afternoon Sunny was standing outside of the stable talking to Jonah when two cowboys came out of the saloon. There was no doubt what they were up to. They were going to have a gunfight, but it took Sunny longer than Jonah to understand it. He tried to steer her away, but at the last minute she realized what was happening.

"Jonah we have to stop them," she yelled as she picked up her skirts and started to run into the street. He grabbed her around the waist and pulled her back, turning her around to face him.

"What do you think you're doing?" he demanded, with the muscle working in his jaw as he gritted his teeth with anger, "Do you want me to carry your dead body home to your father. You can't interfere with two idiots." She was staring at his face when two loud gun blasts went off in quick sequence. She flinched at the sound. She jerked from his arms and turned around. People were gathering around to check out who was still standing and who was down. Two men carried a young cowboy across the street and down the boardwalk to Doc's office.

"Come on, I'll walk you to the general store. You stay there until the crowd thins out, then you get yourself home, fast."

"Why didn't you stop them, Jonah?" she inquired sorrowfully.

"Why should I get my rear end shot off if two fools want to kill each other? You listen and you listen good. This happens here sometimes. You stay out of the way. I don't want to scrape you up off the ground and take you home for your parents to grieve over. If I interfered in every gunfight, I'd already be in the ground. Some things you might change, but a blazing gun isn't going to give you a chance."

"I'm sorry! I can walk myself home." She turned on her heel and crossed the street. He watched her until she turned the corner. He'd been really scared when she started to run into the middle of the trouble. In his mind he saw her life taken from her, so still in death from being shot. He chased the thought away, knowing it had come close to happening.

Clay was on the scene with the young deputy. Jonah walked back inside the smithy where Simon was watching from the doorway.

"Miss Sunny don't understand how mean some people are, does she?" Simon asked as he turned toward Jonah.

"I'm afraid not. She thinks she can save the whole world." He placed his arm across Simon's shoulder and they turned and watched the crowd disperse across the street.

The next day Jonah had shod Edward Clare's horse. The old man was nice, but he always wanted to stand around and chat. He saw Sunny stop outside of the smithy. She waited for a few minutes, then turned and walked back toward the stables. He tried to cut Edward short, but he was hard to get rid of. Simon was at the trading post so he wondered if she stayed or went on down the street. After Edward left, he walked around to the pasture area and saw her leaning over and rubbing Gypsy. Those two sure had taken to each other. He stepped quietly up to the fence and put his foot upon the railing across from where she stood.

"Hi"

"Hi, Jonah"

"Are you still mad at me?"

"I'm not mad. My father thinks you were right and tells me that I should thank you for saving my life," she said, without taking her eyes off of Gypsy.

"No need to thank me."

She looked at him. Her eyes looked sad today. "I hear the cowboy is still alive, and is at Doc's office."

"Clay said he was still over there. He's pretty bad, but he's young. He said those two had been going after each other for awhile, but didn't know what their problem was. He said they've been reading those glorified stories of the old west. These boys should know that most of those gunslingers shoot each other in the back, or ambush them from a hiding place." He paused and waited for her to say something, but she turned back and continued to rub Gypsy's head.

"You're still disappointed in me for not walking in and stopping it, aren't you?" he asked, gently.

"No, I'm not disappointed in you," she answered as she looked at him."

"You look to me like you are," he stated, matter-of-factly.

"No Jonah, I'm not. It's just that you're not born just to exist. We're here to help people. You always act so hard like you don't care for most folks, but you cared for Simon, and rescued him. Some day you'll have a choice put upon you again like that, and will have to get involved. I realize those cowboys were bent on that gunfight. You were right and we might have been hurt, but we could have tried to do something.

"Simon was different. He wasn't in any position to help himself. Both of those boys were old enough to know better, and they made their choice. You can't save the whole world, Sunshine," he said tenderly.

"I know, that's what Papa said. He told me he used to be like me, but he's learned over the years that some things are out of his hands." Jonah wondered if there was some truth to her words. Maybe people weren't born just to exist, but nobody rescued him when he was a kid. He'd never been sorry about stepping in when the odds were uneven, but as a general rule, men didn't really have many brains. If they didn't kill themselves one way, they did it another.

When Sunny left Jonah she stopped in at Doc's on her way home. She knew his last name was Egan, but she didn't think anyone knew his first name because everyone just called him Doc. He was a man of average height, and slender almost to the point of being skinny. He was in his fifties and had brown hair that was almost red, being more prominent in his bushy handlebar mustache. He had mischievous green eyes, an easy smile, and usually had an unlit pipe in his mouth. Sunny liked him immensely

She entered his office. Inside was a waiting room with a few chairs, a large desk, and a big bookshelf along the back wall. That's as far as she ever went. Her father told her he had a medicine room, a six-bed recovery room, and living quarters in the back. Sunny sat down on one of the chairs and decided to wait to see how the cowboy was. She picked up a crumpled newspaper and skimmed through it for a few minutes.

"I thought I heard somebody in here" Doc said, as he came into the room and sat in his swivel chair behind his desk.

"What can I do for you, Missy?" he asked, smiling. He had called her Missy from the first time he met her.

"I saw the gunfight and wondered how the cowboy was," she asked, concerned.

"He's going to live. I will keep him in here for a few days. Maybe he learned a lesson, and the pain will remind him what a fool he is," Doc replied, chuckling.

"I'm glad he's okay. He was really young looking."

"Probably about eighteen or so. If they manage to get older, they usually learn a few things."

"I just wanted to know, Doc. Thanks for telling me," she answered, as she got up from the chair.

"I'm glad you stopped by. I wanted to talk to you. Your father told me you volunteered some nursing time in the hospital in Virginia." he questioned, as he swiveled in his chair.

"Yes, I did. Why?"

"Sometimes, like now, when I have a patient in the ward and have visits to make, I need someone to stay with them. My wife did it for years, until she died three years ago. I haven't had anyone to help since. Would you be interested?"

"Yes, I would, Doc," she said, excitedly. She enjoyed helping in the hospital, and would love to do it again.

"Well we aren't a nice big hospital and I don't always have a patient, but I could use your help part of the time. I can't pay you a lot, but I can give you little pence."

"Oh, Doc I wouldn't even care if you paid me. I loved the nursing I did. I was just learning a little when we moved."

"Okay then. Come by about eight in the morning. Simon usually has my buggy ready by then."

"Doc, thank you!" she exclaimed, as she ran around his desk and kissed him on his cheek.

"Well, I swan, Missy. If I had known I would have made you so all fired happy, I would have asked you sooner," he stated, laughing with pleasure.

"You won't be sorry Doc, I promise, she said, pointing her finger at him, as she left.

"I just bet I won't either," he replied, smiling.

*   *

In the following weeks, Sunny went to Doc's daily. Sometimes she didn't stay long, for there wasn't much for her to do. Other times she was there all day, helping him as he saw patients. He showed her how to organize his cabinets in a certain order like his wife had done. He taught her what to do with patients until he got to them, and what to do in emergencies if he wasn't around, giving her a book to study on how to take care of things from broken bones to bleeding when she was alone in the office. She absorbed everything she read and loved helping him.

They became friends and she felt like he was a favored uncle. He told her that his wife was the only woman he had ever loved. They'd lost a child in their youth and never had another. His wife became his right hand, helping with patients, organizing his important matters, and completing his life. He'd said his biggest sorrow was that he couldn't save her. He tried so hard but he just didn't have the ability.

He later found out that there had been new discoveries in medicine that he didn't know about, and things that might have actually helped if he had known. After her death, and in his grief and guilt, he went back and took a course in new advances in the medical field. He told Sunny that it didn't bring her back, but he hoped to never lose anyone again from ignorance.

He always teased and laughed. Sunny had asked him why he was always so happy, when he saw so much sadness. He told her life was too short to be miserable, since he couldn't lose anything worse than he already had. She soon found out that many people just dropped in on Doc, and if he wasn't busy they just sat and talked. Some people dropped in just to see what she was doing too. She sometimes thought it was a social center instead of a doctor's office. She enjoyed her work and it kept her busy. From Doc's front window she could see Jonah down the street when he stepped out of the smithy to talk to someone. If she wasn't busy she would step out onto the boardwalk and wave to him. She wished he would stop in and see her like the young deputy did. Sunny sometimes watched Jonah from her window and knew her feelings for him were getting deeper. She wondered how he felt about her. Her heart sang with the first bloom of love, but didn't know how tragic that could be.

♥

Chapter 7
Winter-1859- 1860

Jonah hoped that the problems between the North and South would die down, but as fall moved into winter it didn't look much better. He even had some confrontations with people over Simon. Some men accused him of treating him too well. It didn't take Jonah long to put on his gun belt more often. He worried that if something happened to him, Simon wouldn't know what to do, so he gave Clay a paper of ownership in that event.

It was a cold and snowy winter. Sunny wasn't about much, but he could see her come and go into Doc's office. She would sometimes drop by for a few minutes. He and Simon both missed her. He knew she was probably staying in where it was warm, and he didn't blame her. She had gotten over the cowboy being shot, but was glad when he lived and went home. Jonah hoped she would someday learn that bad things happened in this world, and she couldn't change them. Working for Doc might help her understand that better.

There was less business in the winter and the farmers and ranchers were just taking care of their stock. He knew when spring arrived people would want everything done at once. Usually when winter came, he relaxed some. He read or worked on projects that he had. He was restless this year, and he didn't know why. The thought entered his head that maybe it was because he didn't see Sunny as often. He would banish it from his mind as fast as it sneaked in. He thought maybe this was a good thing. He and Simon could get back to normal. Neither of them needed to look forward to her visits.

The young deputy was happier with the winter because Sunny didn't stop by Jonah's so much. Hayden would stop in at Doc's and flirt with her, thinking he was getting closer while she was forgetting Jonah. That pleased him. In his own mind he started thinking of her as his own.

*   *

February brought in a warm spell, and everybody was getting spring fever. They wanted the long winter to be over. Some young cowboys came into town every once in a while to let off steam. They had been pretty well stuck on the ranch during the winter, with the ice, mud and snow. Jonah knew about fighting ice from the water troughs himself.

A young man named Johnny Fry had been hired for the first leg of the journey from St. Jo, for the Pony Express. Rumor had it that the first ride would be mid-March to early April. Jonah stood outside the stables, and felt the sunshine on his face. Maybe winter would soon be over. He was ready for spring. He had a knot of anticipation in his stomach, for he knew Sunny would not let a beautiful day like this pass by. Just as he started to turn and go back inside he spotted Sunny and her mother coming down the street. As they got closer they waved at him. He waited and watched them cross the street as they came over to talk to him.

"Hello, Jonah! Isn't it a beautiful day?" she said with her big smile. He hadn't seen those pretty blue eyes often enough through the cold months. He smiled back and nodded his head. "Sure is. We have been waiting for this all winter. How are you Mrs. Markley?"

"Wonderful. Thanks for asking, and how have you been this winter?"

"Just waitin' for spring, like everybody else."

"Where is Simon?" Sunny questioned, looking around.

"Probably in the trading post. I see Brat on the porch," he said tipping his head in that direction.

"We are headed over there ourselves. We just wanted to say hi," Bess Markley commented.

Sunny reached over and put her hand on Jonah's wrist. "I may come by later. Mom always likes to get her business done and go home. She doesn't like to gossip and gab like I do."

Jonah laughed. Only Sunny would say that about herself. She smiled at him, her eyes twinkling with humor. "I'm like my father in that way, I think. I will talk to you later," she said, as she turned back toward the trading post.

Jonah watched them as they crossed the street, not failing to notice the sway of Sunny's hips. "It must be mating season," he whispered to himself.

*   *

April 3rd was the first run for the Pony Express. Many people stood in the street to see Johnny leave, mounted on his horse Sylph. The crowd waved at him and wished him good luck. He rode out of town with a wave, heading for the ferry that would take him on his way. After a few weeks everybody got used to his weekly ride and the Pony Express captured the hearts and imagination of people all over the world. It was one of the most written about stories in the newspaper. It was America's hero, in the middle of all the problems between the states.

The town was growing by leaps and bounds. Over a million immigrants had come into the United States the year before, and they were settling everywhere. A Chinese man opened a laundry beside the barber shop. An Italian man operated a leather shop, selling fine hand tooled leather products, especially boots. A meat packing place opened.

Sunny and Mack's new wife, Molly became good friends. They met downtown sometimes. Jonah was sure that she probably visited lots of people in town, for it seemed everyone knew her. Even when Molly was with her, she would stop by and say hi to him and Simon. He was busy again with people needing everything fixed for farming and ranching. Isaiah and Sunny were again riding into the country to visit parishioners when she wasn't busy at Doc's, and that made Jonah a little nervous. He didn't think Isaiah carried a gun, and probably didn't know how to use it if he did.

There were still things happening around the country. The Congress couldn't agree on anything, so how could the people? He kept thinking that maybe they could avoid a war. The North seemed to think the South didn't really want to fight, and the South thought the same thing about the North. Jonah just hoped that if it did happen that it wouldn't be bad, or last long.

Jonah finished his work in the smithy, took his leather apron off and hung it on a nail. He poured himself a cup of coffee, and leaned against the door. He saw Clay across the street talking to some cowboys. Soon they got on their horses and left. Clay turned and came across the street to his place.

"Got some coffee for me?"

"Sure thing", he said and poured him a cup. They both stood in the doorway watching people move about on the warm April day.

"Problems?"

"Yeah, four brothers. I had a run in with them a couple of times before. They live on a ranch between here and Independence. They stop here every now and then. The three older boys seem to be okay, but that youngest, the red-headed one, is mouthy and spoiled. The older ones take care of him. He's going to get them all killed one of these days."

"That seems to happen. Either they spoil the youngest, or they have so many they ignore them."

"This one is definitely spoiled. "Clay said, shaking his head.

"How're Marie and the kids?"

"Marie is in the family way," he uttered so quietly that Jonah almost didn't hear what he said. Jonah threw back his head and laughed.

"How old are the girls? Jonah asked, still chuckling.

"Fourteen and eleven." Clay answered meekly.

"At least you will have help raising it," Jonah said, full of mirth.

"I'll have to have all the help I can get. I'll be a doddering old fool before it's raised."

Jonah laughed again. "You're only forty-four. Some men are in their fifties or sixties before they quit having kids."

"I know. I was the middle child of ten. We fought for everything we got. Somebody was always there to take it away from you." Clay explained.

"At least you had something to take away! I had to scrounge and fight the rats for mine. You might get a boy this time."

"Yeah, maybe. Marie and the girls are excited," he said smiling.

Jonah slapped him on the shoulder and smiled. Clay was a good father, and he knew he would love it as much as he did his girls. After he left Jonah threw his remaining coffee on the ground, and went back to work.

Jonah heard Brat bark a greeting, and he knew Sunny was probably outside. He walked around to the fence and saw her rubbing the dog's head and talking to him. Simon was sitting on the fence eating some cookies she brought. Gypsy raised her head and started to wander over toward her. Sunny stepped upon the fence to greet her. Jonah smiled and shook his head. He had never seen a woman bedazzle kids and animals like she did.

"You are distracting my crew, Lady", he said.

"Don't be such an ogre, Jonah. Every hard working person and animal needs a break. I brought some sugar cookies. Want some?"

"Are there any left?" he asked, looking at Simon with a teasing smile.

"I saved you some Jonah," Simon replied, as he passed a cookie to him.

"You sure can cook," Jonah admitted as he took a bite out of it. She smiled at him with satisfaction. Brat interrupted their easy conversation with serious barking.

Jonah stepped over to the edge of the fence to see what the fuss was about.

"Don't move off that fence, Sunny. Run and get my shovel Simon, we have a copperhead in the grass over here."

Simon was back shortly and handed the shovel to Jonah. The dog kept backing up, but wouldn't leave. Jonah stepped in and moved the dog back with the heel of his boot. He took aim and cut the snake's head off with the shovel. He parted the grass and picked it up by the tail. When he held it up, it touched the ground.

Simon whistled. "That's a big one. He's almost as long as you are tall"

"It's plenty long all right."

After burying the snake's head, he walked over to the fence. He then noticed Sunny's look of horror. She was clinging to the fence for dear life. He dropped the snake and walked over and touched her shoulder. She was shaking like a leaf.

"What's the matter? Did that bother you?"

"I'm deathly scared of snakes. Are you sure there aren't any more around?"

"There are no more. You would be smart to watch for them when you're out, even though they are usually in the hills." He pulled her from the fence by her waist and set her on the ground. She threw her arms around his waist and buried her face in his chest. Jonah put his arms around her and soothingly told her everything was all right. She finally quit shaking so much, pulled back and looked up at him.

"Thanks, if I had seen it I think I would have fainted and I have never fainted in my life."

"Are you okay?" Jonah asked, gently.

"Yes," she replied as she shook her head, and slowly pulled out of his arms.

After she left, Jonah went back to the smithy to finish up his work. He didn't have his mind on work; he had it on her being in his arms. How many nights had he thought of that, but the real thing beat fantasies all to pieces. He really needed to distance himself from her, but it got harder all of the time.

Hayden standing across the street saw Sunny in Jonah's arms, and didn't like it one bit. He didn't know what to do about it but he needed to do something.

The moon shone into his bedroom window, but he knew that wasn't the reason he couldn't sleep. Jonah got up, put his Levi's on and walked out into the cool night. He sat down on the railing of the porch. The woman had him in a bad state. His body had betrayed him before, but this time his mind and heart were involved. When he first saw her he was intrigued. When he met her he was interested and now that he knew her, he was falling in love.

"Falling, that's bull. I'm already lost," he said to himself, quietly. He wanted her; she made him feel alive when she was near. He wanted to hold her and love her. She had shown him how to love life, and he hadn't even realized that until each time when she left his presence. He didn't think he was capable of loving like she did, and he certainly knew he could never have her.

She loved life, people, and even dumb animals. She would make someone an extraordinary wife. What a mother she would be. He knew he wanted to marry her, but it was out of the question. Even if she agreed, how long would it be before she woke up disappointed in her choice when people wouldn't speak to her and snubbed her because she was married to a half-breed? It would kill him each time he looked into her eyes and saw the love of life gone. He knew he couldn't ever go any further than friendship with her and he could live with that. He would look forward to seeing Sunny, and when she married someone, someday, memories of her for the rest of his life would be his reward. It was more than he ever expected.

All he had to do is never give in to his feelings and to remember that, above all. Noticing the night sky and seeing all the stars twinkling, he knew Sunny noticed that kind of beauty too. It made him feel close to her. If he was honest, that would be his wish, to have her with him forever. He was going to lose her, and soon losing Simon was also in the future. The boy was growing up and would want to go find his family. He was already talking about fighting in the war so he could help free the slaves. Jonah shuddered every time he mentioned it. He was afraid for him, yet knew he couldn't stand in his way. He would probably do the same thing in his shoes. Jonah was hoping somebody came up with an answer before this whole country went crazy. He was afraid when the smoke cleared, if he was still standing, he'd be alone, like most of his life.

Jonah was busy with some little things he had been putting off when he noticed the smithy got dark. Someone had shut the door. He turned around and laid down his hammer. The young deputy was standing in the doorway, looking incensed.

"Can I help you Hayden?" Jonah asked, looking at him with a hard stare.

"Yeah you can. You can stay away from Miss Sunny. I saw you hugging her right in plain sight yesterday. You're a half-breed, and you're not good enough for her," he said, tight lipped.

"You're right Hayden, I'm not good enough for her, and I'm the first to admit it. But let me tell you youngster, you're not good enough for her either."

"At least I'm white."

Jonah walked over close to him, leaning down to his height. "Do you think being white is the only requirement for a husband? You need to be a man, and you're a long way from that. You're like a little kid that pouts when he doesn't get his way. You're only thinking of what you want. If you really cared for Sunny you might consider what she wants," Jonah commanded, enunciating each word clearly.

"I suppose you think she wants you."

"It wouldn't matter, Hayden, if she wanted me or not. I would never subject her to a life with me when there are too many people like you in the world."

"What do you mean by that," he replied, defiantly.

"You and your kind think anybody different than you are worthless. Blacks, Indians, Irish, German. It doesn't matter to you because as far as you're concerned we are all less than human. We may be harder workers, more intelligent, more tolerant, more caring, more of a real human being, but because we don't have white skin, or the right background, we are nothing in your eyes," Jonah said, barely suppressing his buried anger.

Hayden whirled away from Jonah and headed to the door.

"Hayden!"

He stopped and turned back.

"Just so you know, I don't chase after Sunny. She stops in here on her own when she feels like it, just like she visits with everyone else in town. I'm not a problem for you or anyone else." Jonah stated, firmly.

Without saying a word, Hayden threw the door open, spilling light back into the smithy.

After locking up, Jonah headed over to see Clay. He was still mad and needed to hash out his feelings with him. He stomped into the office and took a chair across from him.

Clay watched him cross the room and sit down. He knew his friend well enough to know that when he took his hat off and slammed it across his knees, there was a problem.

"Somethin' wrong?" he asked, waiting for Jonah to speak.

"Yeah. I just had a visit from Hayden. Seems he thinks I'm not good enough for Sunny. Of course I know that's true, and I agreed with him. I don't know what I'm so danged mad about. Maybe because he had the gall to tell me that to my face, or the fact that it makes me so furious that this good for nothing world dictates everybody's life. I should be used to that by now. Clay, I think I have a fury buried in me that I can't tamp down sometimes," he exclaimed, dropping his head down, looking at the floor, turning his hat rapidly in his hands.

Clay got up and moved around and sat on the edge of his desk.

"Jonah you're about the best man I know. I have a fury about all this injustice too. It frustrates me so much sometimes I want to punch some people in the jaw. I might just do that to Hayden to make me feel better."

Jonah slapped his hat back on his head. "Nah, don't do that. He's not the only person that feels that way. I'm not trying to get him into trouble. He's right though. I thought if Sunny came by on her own like she has been, that it would be okay. But it's only going to get worse. Hayden probably isn't the only person that has noticed her hanging over my fence talking to me and Simon. Sunny's going to face problems about it if she keeps coming around, no getting around it." He sighed heavily, then added "Tell Doc to talk to Isaiah, and ask her not to come by anymore".

"Is that what you really want?"

"What does what I want have to do with anything?" Jonah asked, furiously.

"Are you sorry that you met her?"

Jonah looked at Clay with all the anger gone from his face. "Never. I have never known anyone like her. I will love her forever, no matter what happens. I will live on the swatches of memories that she gave me. Just talk to Doc, I can't let her suffer humiliation because of me. "

After Clay patted him on the shoulder, he promised he would. Jonah turned and left.

Clay would go talk to Doc as soon as he gave Hayden a bloody nose.

♥

Chapter 8

Sunny was peeling apples at the table, while her mother sliced them for an apple pie. Deep in thought, she was not keeping her mind on her chore.

"Mama, how did you know when you first loved Papa?" she asked, softly.

"I knew I liked him when I first met him. As I got to know him my affection grew, until one day I had no doubt," her mother answered looking gently at her daughter. "Why do you ask?"

"I don't know, I just wondered?"

"Is this about Jonah?"

Sunny looked at her mother, "What made you say that?" she asked, laying her paring knife down in the bowl of peeled apples.

"You treat him differently than you do most people. You have always been a friendly and outgoing person, but you show no interest except friendship in the young deputy or the other men that seek you out."

"How do I treat him differently?" Sunny responded, looking at her mother for the answer she already knew.

"It's the way you look at him. Your tone of voice has a different sound and your smile is more enticing. Your eyes are softer and sparkle with delight. You can tell that just being around him makes you happier."

"Oh Mama, I think you're right. I always thought that I would never marry until I loved someone as much as you cared for Papa. People call him hard and tough, but I see other things in him. He always says he's not the marrying kind. I feel like he cares sometimes, but he doesn't show it. I think I will just have to wait and see what develops," she said unhappily.

Sunny knew she loved Jonah, but thought it was going to take a lot for him to admit how he felt about her. He didn't show his emotions often, but when he held her the other day she was sure it was tighter than he needed to.

She didn't ever want to let go of him, but she thought she should before he guessed her feelings.. He was worth waiting for.

*　　*

The boys were back and the youngest one was mouthing off as usual. Jonah stood and watched from the smithy. Clay was trying to talk the young one into putting his gun away. He challenged a farmer from the area into a gunfight. The three older brothers were standing behind him, ready to help if the need arose. They didn't look as though their hearts were in it.

Clay must have told the farmer to get on his horse and leave because he hurried to his horse, mounted it, and rode out. The kid took his hat off and waved it in the air with a great show as he pointed his finger at Clay. Jonah couldn't make out what was being said, but he could see the kid was mad. Before he replaced his hat, Jonah noticed he had bright red hair. He was a lot smaller than his brothers. He wondered if that was part of the kid's problem, trying to show that he was as good as his bigger older brothers.

All at once, things seemed to change. The kid drew his gun on Clay. Jonah picked up his rifle from the wall, where he kept it, loaded. He didn't waste time. He rushed across the street to back Clay up. He slung his rifle into position, taking a stance beside his friend.

"Maybe two firearms are needed here," he announced, looking coldly at the kid. Watching the older brothers from the corner of his eye, he waited for some move.

"Come on, Howie, put the gun away. It's time to go home." One of the brothers said.

"Okay, we will give you a break this time," the kid said, looking back and forth from Clay to Jonah.

"I think maybe you did yourself a favor, son. You would have been pushing up daisies," Jonah replied, callously.

The kid visibly flinched, then tried to cover it with a tough manner. He returned his gun to his holster and motioned to his brothers to leave. They all mounted their horses and left.

"For a minute there, I thought I had put myself in a sticky situation. Thanks for backing me up. I won't take it so lightly the next time," Clay said as he slapped Jonah on the shoulder.

"Think nothing of it. That kid is like a copperhead just waiting to strike."

"I think you're right," Clay replied, as the men walked across the street to Jonah's place. Jonah replaced his rifle on the wall.

"I think the kid's wanting a gunfight but he's a little afraid he might not win so he picks on farmers and old men. He feels intimidated by his older brothers. They are all bigger and stronger than he is. Because he was small the whole family probably looked out for him. Have you ever watched his brothers? They don't really get into it; they just stand behind him in case he needs help." Jonah explained.

"They need to kick his butt. That would probably do more good than to stand there and help him make a mess." Clay said, as he took a seat on a nail keg.

"You're right. If his brothers weren't standing behind him, he wouldn't be in such a hurry to pull that fancy gun on people."

"He always picks a fight with somebody that he thinks has never shot anything bigger than a rabbit. He will make a big mistake one of these days."

"Did you talk to Doc?" Jonah asked, as he took a seat.

"Yeah, but Doc thinks everything would be okay, if he or Isaiah accompanied her when she came to see you. He doesn't think she would listen to him anyway. She has a mind of her own."

"You need to convince her. I don't think Hayden will let up, and soon he will bring everybody's attention to it."

"He won't be saying much for awhile. His mouth is swollen."

Jonah wrinkled his forehead as he looked at Clay "You didn't, did you?"

"Couldn't help it old friend. I was so dad-blamed mad that I hit him right in the middle of yelling at him."

Jonah burst out laughing. "I wish I could have got my swing in too." He knew it wouldn't help anything, but it made him feel better.

Sunny was in the kitchen helping her mother with supper, when her father came in the back door. He poured himself a cup of coffee and sat at the table.

"Sunny, I need to talk to you about something," he said, as he picked up his coffee to take a sip.

"What is it, Papa? You look serious," she answered, as she pulled out a kitchen chair and sat down.

"Doc stopped me on the street today. He wanted to tell me that the young deputy saw you the other day all snuggled in Jonah's arms. He's spouting off about that half-breed hugging you right in plain sight. Clay gave him a big lecture on keeping his mouth shut, but he doesn't think that's going to make much difference. Doc says he's going to cause you problems and that I need to talk to you."

"That was the day he killed the snake. I was scared, so I grabbed him. That's all it was. Besides it's nobody's business."

Isaiah reached across and took his daughter's hand, and gently said, "People around here think it's their business, especially now, when we are right on the verge of a war over such a big controversy."

"Papa, I love Jonah. I have never loved anyone before, but I promise I haven't done anything wrong."

"You may have to forget how you feel about him. It can only cause problems."

"Papa, you aren't like that. You like Jonah. Why are you lecturing me on my emotions?"

"If you hang around Jonah anymore things are going to get worse. The deputy is not even the worst narrow-minded person around here."

"I don't care what those people think."

"You had better care, Sunny. You might be willing to live in a community where nobody will speak to you or have anything to do with you. The problem is you are putting Jonah's life in danger. There are people here that would drag him into the middle of the street and hang him for messing with a white girl." Sunny gasped and covered her mouth. Her eyes were big and round. She realized what her father was saying. She had heard of such things before, but she hadn't even thought of that. Tears swam in her eyes.

Isaiah got up and reached over pulling his daughter into his arms. "I'm sorry. You know I have no problem with Jonah. He's a fine man, but we are in a place and time where it's almost impossible. If you want to visit Jonah, you wait for me to go with you. If I am along, nobody can say anything. I am warning you though, if you love Jonah, it's not going to make things any easier being around him."

"Okay, Papa; I will be more cautious, and take somebody with me. I wouldn't care though if it wasn't for Jonah's safety. She just couldn't understand how hateful people could be.

*   *

Molly Reeves became Sunny's best friend when she married Mack and moved into town. She visited her almost everyday and sometimes they went downtown together. Molly was more reserved than Sunny, but they got along well. She admired the friendly personality that Sunny had, making friends out of perfect strangers. Molly had lived in St. Jo most of her life, but it seemed like Sunny knew as many people as she did.

A new family, John and Ruthy Fults, moved to a small farm a few miles out of town. They spent most of the spring building their house and trying to get their ground ready for crops. The church people and some close neighbors decided to go out on Saturday and raise their barn. The women were going to cook, and when the building was finished, they would have a barn dance. Sunny and Molly looked forward to it. This would be a way to forget all the country's problems. Sunny hoped Jonah and Simon were going.

Saturday, Sunny and her parents went to the farm. Men were busy building the barn when they arrived. Isaiah joined them while Sunny and her mother went into the house to help cook. She noticed Jonah among the men with Simon working beside him.

She took a minute to watch them swing their hammers, nailing boards to the frame that was already up. She turned around and followed her mother into the house. Molly was preparing some apple pies and Sunny went over to help her.

"How many are we making?" Sunny asked as she tied a towel around her waist.

"Several, I think. I'm not sure everyone is here. Some more may show up yet."

"They look like they have done quite a bit already."

"Some were here early. Mack wanted to get here before anyone so that he could get the frame done right."

"I saw Jonah and Simon, but I didn't notice Mack."

"He's probably checking everybody's work. He thinks everything has to be perfect, even a barn," she said, smiling with pride.

When she and Molly finished baking the pies and had them cooling, they went onto the porch. They couldn't believe how far they had come in just a couple of hours. Some more people arrived. Women came in with even more food. They sat down on the porch railing, while a few of the older women sat on the swing. They were complimenting Mrs. Fults on the new house that they had just finished. It smelled of new wood.

The girls turned around to watch the workers. Sunny noticed Mack working, and Molly watching him. She knew they loved each other by the way they acted together. Sunny wanted that kind of love. She watched Jonah, who stood out among all the men, knowing her feelings for him made her admire him. She couldn't control her heart, no matter what other people thought. He never told her in words what she wanted to hear. He just kept claiming that he wasn't the marrying kind, and maybe he truly meant it. She thought maybe he didn't feel the freedom to marry, because of his heritage. Sunny was heartsick over the conversation with her father. If it wasn't for putting Jonah's life in danger she would thumb her nose to everybody and continue to see him. But she would die if anything happened to Jonah, and especially if she had caused it.

"You like Jonah don't you?" asked Molly.

"Yes, I do, a lot. In fact I'm not sure it stops at liking," she said quietly.

"Mack says he's a good man."

"I know he is, but I am dreaming dreams that are not possible," she said, with a sigh, and told her friend what her father had said.

"I can understand your problem. People are cruel. Mack and I would speak to you no matter who you married, but your papa is right. It might put his life in danger."

After finishing the barn around four, everyone was starving. Women brought out food to a makeshift table soon covered with pork, fried chicken, potatoes, beans, loaves of bread, and home churned butter. Various cakes, pies, cookies and puddings filled the table. Everybody heaped their plates and made short order of the food. Kids were running around with chicken legs in their hands, playing while eating.

Sunny's eyes kept searching out Jonah. He sat beside Simon on the ground with Mack and a few other men. After everyone ate and rested, and the women cleaned up everything, a couple of older men got out fiddles and stringed instruments and announced that it was time to dance. Men, women and children started filing into the barn.

Sunny saw Jonah standing with some men talking. She thought about walking near them when Hayden grabbed her for a partner. As she was dancing in the crowd she kept looking for Jonah in her whirling sight. When the dance was over she thanked Hayden and he walked her to where her parents were standing. Sheriff Clay and his wife, Marie, were talking to them. She said "hello" to them, and joined in the conversation.

She looked for Jonah, but he wasn't around. She knew he and Simon had left.

A few days later she rode Gypsy down the street with her father beside her.

He started coming with her when she wanted to visit Jonah. Sometimes Doc and she walked down together. They rode onto a side street where there wasn't much activity.

"Papa, is Jonah mad at me?" she asked.

"I don't think so, honey. Clay probably informed him of the trouble that was brewing with the deputy."

"He was almost unfriendly to me today."

"I don't think he was mad at you." he answered, as they turned the corner and headed up the adjoining street. A woman was shaking a rug out, and watched them ride by. People in the neighborhood were used to seeing Sunny riding.

"Maybe I shouldn't come by so much."

"I told you, it's not making things easier"

"Oh, Papa, why is life so complicated?" she sighed.

"We live in a complicated world right now. Our country is splitting in half over all the rights and wrongs of people. St. Jo is divided right down the middle over the issues plaguing our country."

Jonah was excited to see Sunny, but he was mad at himself for how his heart jumped when she came into sight. He decided to be a little reserved for his own good and knew she noticed, for she looked at him a little hurt.

She asked if she could ride Gypsy, and he told her yes, if someone went along with her. Jonah went back to work and ignored her. Sunny and Isaiah left the stables for a ride. He stood against the door of the smithy and saw them coming back down the street. He moved back into the shadows and watched them dismount and take the horses into the stables. Soon afterwards she and her father left and walked down the board walk. That wasn't like Sunny, and he knew it was all about the deputy seeing them together. Doc told him she didn't care who saw her, until her father explained to her about putting his life in danger. He told Doc he could take care of himself, never to tell her that again. He could not let her protect him. He knew he had to talk to her. It was the end of May, the wildflowers were out, and the sky was blue. Sunny hadn't been by in a couple of weeks. He felt empty when she didn't drop in. He had been watching for her for several days, and he hadn't seen her except from a distance coming and going into Doc's office. But finally, today, he was about to pour himself a cup of coffee when he saw her coming down the street. She stopped to talk to a couple on the street for a few minutes. That was his opportunity to be waiting for her when she got to the general store.

He was leaning against the post when she walked up.

"I want to talk to you" he said, firmly

"Okay, if you wish," she replied as she looked at him with her clear blue eyes. He took her by the arm and walked her across the street to the smithy. When they entered she turned to him, waiting for him to say what he wanted.

"I haven't seen you in a while," he said gently as he touched her shoulder.

"You acted mad at me. I didn't need an invitation to leave. I got the message," she said defiantly. Jonah smiled broadly. Her eyes dared him to come up with some lame excuse.

"Come on, Sweetheart. Can't I have a bad day?"

"You can have all you want if you don't take it out on your friends."

"Are you going to punish me forever?" he asked, as he moved his hand toward her elbow. He couldn't stop touching her.

"Probably," she answered with her nose in the air but with a small mischievous smile on her lips.

"You're going to make me say it, aren't you?" he questioned, amused.

She put her hands on her hips, looking him straight in the eyes. "Yes, I am. Say, I miss you, I didn't mean to hurt your feelings, and please, please, please, come back and visit any time you want." He repeated it word for word, chuckling through the whole sentence and drawing please out as long as she had. She laughed too.

"I wanted to talk to you. I don't want you to worry about me getting hurt. I can take care of myself, but you need to remember that people will cause you trouble if you are seen with me. I don't know how far the deputy will take all this. I don't want you snubbed by anyone.

"Jonah, how can I not worry about you? There are those kinds of people around here. I won't put your life in danger."

"I won't put yours in danger either, so it's best that we don't make it easy for anyone."

"Are you saying I can't see you anymore?"

"No, just not as much and never by yourself like now. You should get back to Doc's before someone notices us."

"I can't believe people are so cruel. What difference should it make to them who I am friends with?"

"It does. Maybe it won't always be this way. We can only hope."

Sunny walked straight into his arms, putting her arms around him, "I missed you," she whispered in his ear. He pulled her closer to him.

"I missed you too, Sweetheart." Pulling her from his arms and sending her away was the hardest thing he had ever done.

*   *

Summer 1860

Jonah noticed the smoke on the horizon. It was closer than usual. Bleeding Kansas was a term that had been used for the last few years, since the border wars had started. Kansas was against slavery and the border ruffians were busy at work trying to change that. They wiped out farms and sometimes towns trying to rid Kansas of Northern support. Usually, if there was smoke it was barely seen in St. Joseph. Today it looked like it was as close as Leavenworth. Jonah stepped out to take a closer look and a crowd of people were gathered to see.

"Looks like ole Quantrill is getting closer to us," said Joseph, as Jonah walked up to stand beside him.

"Somethin's happening mighty close. Think we ought to take a ride out that way?"

"Probably so. Wonder where Clay is?"

"You look for him and I'll saddle some horses."

Jonah and Simon just finished getting a few horses ready when Joseph arrived with Clay and a few other men. Strapping their guns on and loading their rifles they left to investigate. They rode less than twenty miles when they came upon a burning farm.

Other people were there from neighboring towns to see what happened.

Jonah had never seen such a sight. It made him weak just to look at it. The house and outbuildings were still burning, but the family lay scattered. They had been shot several times each. Their bloody bodies were strewn about and they all had been scalped. There were five

62

children. The oldest didn't look any older than twelve, and the youngest was about three. There was nothing more to do but bury them. Some people from Atchison identified them as the Eastman family. At least they could put a name on their crude wooden markers.

Jonah knew these things had been going on for some time, but this was the first bit of handiwork he had seen by Quantrill and his band of cutthroats. Anger rushed through him. How did people justify doing such things to other human beings? They all got shovels and began the work of burying innocent people whose only crime was their difference of opinion.

It took Jonah days to get the scene of the murdered family out of his mind. The only thing that occupied it besides that was Sunny. It scared him spitless to think about something like that happening to her. She was so open about how she felt. What if she ran across the wrong person and voiced her beliefs? He shuddered to think what someone would do to her.

It seemed to Jonah that he stepped outside the smithy twenty times a day just to see if he could get a glimpse of her. She started sweeping Doc's porch more often than usual. Looking for him as much as he watched for her. A couple of times, she walked over with Doc, and their eyes said what they weren't allowed to.

If only he could court her properly. If only he could protect her every hour of the day. Too many only ifs. It was just another big joke that life played on him. Where was Sunny's God? He sure had never been around for him. Where was He when Quantrill raided the farm in Kansas last week? He tried to understand Sunny's complete faith in God, but he just couldn't.

He assumed someone would kill him someday, and never really cared that much. Now he wanted to live, wanted to love, and one was certainly not possible.

♥

Chapter 9

Jonah jumped at every little noise on the street for weeks after the Kansas family had been killed. But today, Jonah was busy, so he didn't pay any attention to the ruckus. He gave no attention to the usual noise on the street, hearing some yelling, thinking it was nothing new. It happened from time to time. He was almost finished forming some horseshoes over the forge when Simon came running in.

"Jonah, somebody took Miss Sunny, he yelled, stumbling over his words and out of breath.

He dropped his work and turned to him. "What are you talking about?" he asked, anxiously.

"She was walking down the street and some man rode his horse right up to the boardwalk, chased her down and carried her away."

Jonah's throat went dry from fear. He jerked his apron off and buttoned up his shirt, "Did anybody see who did it?" he questioned, waiting for Simon to tell him more.

"The deputy is getting a posse together to go look for her."

Jonah knew that Clay had boarded a train to Independence early this morning; to take a prisoner back.

Just as Jonah reached for his gun belt, Isaiah came rushing in. "Will you saddle my horse, Jonah? Somebody took my daughter and I want to ride with the posse to find her," he said, frantically.

Jonah turned to him, putting his hands on his shoulders.

"Isaiah, go home and get her a change of clothes and a blanket. I will get us some horses ready and we will go after her. The young deputy probably can't trail a herd of elephants." He leaned in closer, "I promise you, we won't come back without her. Get her things and meet me back here. I will get supplies together and be waiting for you. Hurry!" Stopping in midstep he turned back and asked Isaiah "Do you know what kind of horse he's riding, and what he looks like?"

"All they said was he was a redhead riding…"

"A bay," Jonah interrupted. "I know who he is; Clay has had problems with him before. Which way did he head?"

"North, toward Marysville."

"Hurry, Isaiah," he said, as he dashed across the room to take his rifle down. He turned to Simon.

"Run home and get me some dried beef, hardtack and coffee. Get enough for a few days at least. I will saddle Warrior and Chico and wait for you and Isaiah. Hurry son"

Simon left running as fast as he could go.

It had been trying to rain all day so he decided to take some rain slickers for them. He packed them into the saddlebags and went to saddle his big sturdy horse. Warrior could go for miles without getting winded. By the time he put on his gun belt and packed everything he needed, Isaiah and Simon were back.

"Simon, I won't be back until I find her so you will have to run the stables and take care of things.

"I will, Jonah!"

"You be careful. If you have a problem go to Joseph or Doc."

"I will, Jonah. Don't worry."

"Let's go, Isaiah!"

Sunny couldn't believe this was happening to her. They stopped a few miles from town and the man let her get off of the horse. He was watching through the trees to see if anybody was following them. A short time later a group of horses raced by, going toward Marysville. They didn't turn off onto the trail they were riding. Sunny started screaming and running toward them. "Help me," she yelled, as she continued to run. She heard him chasing her on his horse. Limbs were slapping as he came closer upon her. Sunny continued to scream as she ran for the edge of the trees, hoping someone would hear her. The man jumped from his horse and threw himself upon her, throwing her to the ground, and knocking the wind out of her.

"You had better shut your trap if you know what's good for you," he sneered.

She smelled his hot foul breath as he jerked her to her feet and tied his kerchief across her mouth. He jerked her hands behind her back and tied them together.

"Oh God, help me!"

He hauled her up onto the horse and they took off on down the tree lined trail, leading to, who knew where?

Her mind frantically tried to sort out what she could do to save herself, for she knew he meant to do her harm. With her hands tied she couldn't come up with any solution. Surely he would untie her at some point. If only she could find something to fight him with. Maybe by then somebody would find them. She had to believe someone was looking for her.

It seemed like they had been riding for hours when he finally stopped and shoved her to the ground. She lay where she fell. She felt like crying; but she would not give him the satisfaction of seeing her vulnerable. He jerked her up by the arm and dragged her into some kind of filthy cabin.

"Now you will find out what you were made for lady," he said as he shoved her onto the bed and proceeded to tie her hands to an old rusty bedpost. Sunny began to fight with all of the strength she had, but in just seconds she knew she was going to lose this battle.

Oh, Jonah, I need you!

He couldn't afford to make a mistake; Jonah had to take it slow enough to know where they were headed. Leading his horse, he backtracked and looked for the signs that led onto the boardwalk. Squatting down and looking, Jonah noticed the horse had a very small chip out of the right front shoe. That was going to help, so he mounted his horse and they headed out of town. Getting down from his horse often to check for tracks, he saw where the posse had followed Sunny's abductor out of town. The horses they rode made it almost impossible to find what he was looking for, but finally picked up on the chipped shoe.

He and Isaiah rode for an hour or so, without talking much. They both had a lot on their mind. Jonah had never been so scared, and was sure Isaiah felt the same. Sunny was so full of life and innocent of all the evil things in the world. He had to make it to her as soon as possible. He spotted the posse's tracks leaving the road turning toward Marysville. Jonah just didn't quite believe the kid had gone that way. He figured he would go into the hills where he wouldn't run into many people, or take her to his house, wherever that may be. He kept on the road and soon discovered a horseshoe print with a chipped notch in it.

Rain started to sprinkle. Soon the trail turned into the hills, following the river. They had a harder time in the thick trees, but soon picked up the tracks again when the trees thinned out. As he rode searching for the signs he needed to guide him to Sunny, he tried to keep his emotions in check. He was scared. She had told him he wasn't born just to exist, and one day something would happen that he would have to make a choice to get involved. She was sure right. This was the someday. He would die saving her, if that's what it took. "Hang on sweetheart, I'm coming. I just hope I'm not too late," he said quietly to himself, his heart full of emotion.

They rode for a couple of hours. Jonah knew Isaiah was not used to riding so hard, but there was no way he could have talked him into staying behind, so he didn't even try. He stopped and waited for him.

"How are you doing?"

"It's hard, but I don't want you to slow down on account of me. If I can't keep up, you just keep going. I will find you sooner or later."

Jonah nodded. "Looks like the rain's not goin' to give up. We might just as well get our slickers on now."

He dug them out of the saddlebags and got them a piece of jerky to tide them over for a bit. They took the time to drink some water and then slipped the slickers on. They remounted and started off again. He knew Isaiah's body was screaming, but the need to find his daughter was pressing harder.

The rain went from a downpour back to a steady sprinkling. Jonah was getting concerned, thinking he had missed something. Then he heard a horse whinny a short distance away. Jonah dismounted and took his rifle with him. He moved his horse into a clump of trees and motioned for Isaiah to follow him.

"I heard something. I want you to stay with the horses. I don't want to scare him off, so I'm going to go on foot. Don't come up until you hear me give you a signal, or I get back."

Isaiah nodded to him and tied the horses to a tree branch. Jonah started through the thicket. He hoped daylight held out until he could check things out. He hadn't gone far when he walked through the trees and saw a horse standing by an old rundown lean-to. Walking quietly through the trees he heard a movement behind some bushes. The kid walked into view. Jonah knew he was too late. The kid looked too self-satisfied. There were deep scratches on his cheek and he knew they were from Sunny fighting him off. It made Jonah sick to think of her being overpowered by that lowlife. Hatred like he had never felt ran through him. His body burned with it.

The kid didn't see Jonah until he almost walked into his rifle. He stopped in shock and looked into the coldest eyes he had ever seen.

"Where's the woman?" Jonah demanded, snarling the words out through his clenched teeth.

"What woman," the kid answered, swallowing hard.

"Don't play games with me. Where is she?" he inquired, coldly.

"Inside. She's okay."

"Did you hurt her?" Jonah asked, growling his question harshly.

"Naw, she's okay." The kid answered, visibly shaken.

Jonah stepped closer. "Don't lie to me. Did you violate her?"

"She's not hurt," he whined.

"You picked the wrong woman. What kind of low down scum are you to force yourself on a young woman in a smelly broken down old building?"

He stepped closer and the boy stumbled backward, visibly trembling.

"But I will give you a better chance than you gave her," Jonah said as he pushed the kid farther back with the barrel of his gun. "We can have a gunfight, right here. You have a gun belt on. Just back up ten paces and we will get this started." He gritted his teeth with anger. The kid showed a half-hearted, nervous smile.

"You might want to reconsider. I'm pretty fast. Why don't I just ride off and you can have the woman."

"Back up, now," Jonah shouted, as he laid the rifle on the ground, knowing he would use his pistol for this. They both backed up, and the kid drew without warning, but didn't even clear his holster when Jonah shot him. The lad fell to the ground, grabbing himself around the chest, groaning.

"Help me, Mister… please. I'm sorry I hurt the… woman," he said, struggling to get the words out. Jonah stood there with no remorse, wishing he could shoot him a hundred times. He knew the kid wouldn't last long, and Jonah wanted to watch him die, but getting to Sunny was more important. He replaced his gun, picked up his rifle and went into the rundown shack. Sunny was lying on an old cot with her wrists tied to the bed. She was lying on her side, in a fetal position. Her hair covered her face; the dress was torn, covered with filth. Cringing at what she had gone through, Jonah took his knife out and cut the rope binding her wrist. Sunny let out a cry of fear, but didn't move. He sat on the bed and gently gathered her into his arms.

"Jonah," she whispered, as she buried her face into his chest, sobbing. He held her close, as tears threatened his eyes too. The kid hurt her so badly, taking her innocence in such a brutal way. He wished he had beaten the life out of him before killing him. Jonah rubbed her back and talked with soothing words, knowing they didn't make any sense to either one of them. Not being able to tell her it was okay, because it wasn't. He couldn't tell her she would be over it in time, because she might not. Jonah couldn't say anything that she didn't know better than he, so he finally told her to cry as long as she needed to. His place would be right beside her.

Jonah felt the wetness on his shirt from her tears. He felt guilty that he hadn't gone to see what the ruckus was about, because he might have saved her if he had. Jonah harbored just as much guilt for not finding her in time. It wasn't fair that she had been hurt so, always trusting everyone. Sunny and her family were what good people were really supposed to be like. Her sobbing slowly began to subside, but she kept her face against his chest, with hands clasped tightly to his shirt. She began to loosen her grip. Jonah continued to rub her back and hold her tightly.

"He hurt me, Jonah," she uttered without moving a muscle.

"I know, Sweetheart," he stated, as he kissed the side of her face closest to his cheek.

"I tried to fight him," she whimpered, softly, as she still hid her face, "but then he tied my hands behind my back."

"I know."

"It was so horrible. I wish I could have died."

"I wish I could have saved you," he said, holding her tighter.

"Nobody will forgive me for this." Sunny declared.

"None of this was your fault." Tears were dropping from her eyes, and her chin was shaking. He pulled her back against him and let her cry again.

Neither of them spoke for some time, but she had continued to lie against him, and he continued to comfort her, in the only way he knew how.

They both jumped as Isaiah came rushing into the shack. Isaiah took Sunny from Jonah and she started crying on her father's shoulder, as tears dripped from his eyes too.

"I would like to get her home before morning, Isaiah, if you're both up to the trip. I don't think the rain is going to let up, and if she's home before daylight people will think we got her home soon after she was taken," Jonah said, knowing he had to think about practical things.

"If I arrive before morning, nobody will know my terrible secret, will they?"

"No, they won't," he said, quietly.

"Where is he?"

"Dead!" She raised her head and looked in his eyes questionably.

"Did you kill him?"

Jonah saw no reason to lie to her after all she had been through. He nodded his head, yes.

"Will you go to jail?" she asked, anxiously, her eyes searching his.

"No, I made him draw on me first. I will talk to Clay when we get back."

"I'm glad he's dead. I have never hated anybody, but I hate him," she said, looking at her father.

"It's okay to feel that way now," her father said, knowing he was feeling the same thing.

"You have every right, Sweetheart," Jonah said, as calmly as possible, trying to hide his own anger.

She laid her head against her father's chest and timidly said, "I need to bathe before we leave. May I?" she asked, as she looked up at Jonah.

"Can she?" Isaiah asked, looking at him too.

"Sure. We will keep watch. The water is going to be cold. You can use your dress for your needs; your father brought you another one."

Jonah and Isaiah followed her to the river, and waited with their backs turned until she splashed into the water. He knew the river must be cold, but she probably wasn't feeling that after what she had been through. The two men didn't talk. They both felt ill at ease, having their own thoughts, but were unable at the moment to express them. Jonah knew they would like to kick something hard

71

to get their frustrations out. Killing the kid didn't help. He wished he had tortured him instead.

He stayed beside the river with his rifle. Isaiah gathered some wood, started a small campfire, and put some coffee on. She would need to warm up from the cold water. When she finished, she went behind the bush and dried off with her worn dress, and changed into the fresh one. Sunny walked over to the campfire and sat on the grass behind the fire. Isaiah wrapped the blanket and slicker around her and poured her a hot cup of coffee. Jonah gave them some jerky and hardtack, and then took some for himself with his coffee. Keeping his rifle close, he sat beside them. He wanted to hold her until he healed her, but he knew that was going to take a long time.

"What are you going to do with his body," Isaiah asked.

"Leave it for the buzzards." Jonah proclaimed harshly.

Sunny's eyes met his, understanding.

"It's near dark. Are we going to travel at night?" Isaiah asked.

"It's not that hard. We'll go slowly enough. Warrior has done it before. The problem is that I think we are going to have rain all night. That's going to hide the stars, but we will be okay."

When they got ready to leave Jonah unsaddled the kid's horse, dumped the gear on the ground and slapped the horse on the rump. The bay took off into the woods. Jonah walked over to Warrior and slipped his rifle into the scabbard of his saddle.

"Why didn't you keep the horse for Sunny to ride?" Isaiah questioned.

"Sunny isn't in good enough shape to ride. Besides we don't want any questions why we have the horse until Clay can take care of things. You're going to have a hard enough time just riding, so I will take Sunny up with me. Warrior can handle both of us."

He mounted his big horse, and reached down for Sunny, pulling her in front of him.

"Settle back against me, I'll keep you safe. If you get uncomfortable, let me know, and we'll stop and rest."

She snuggled against him, and they started for home, traveling slowly. The sky darkened, and it began sprinkling. Jonah covered Sunny's head up with the hood of the slicker. Rain dropped slowly on his hat and ran off of the back and sides when he tipped his head. They rode deep into the woods where it became especially dark. They slowed down and watched carefully. Jonah couldn't see much but the outline of the trees. He wished he had Brat along. The dog would have been a help, but he always left him with Simon. He listened for Isaiah behind him. He was keeping up, never complaining. His daughter's needs came first.

Sunny never said a word, but he knew she wasn't asleep, for she would stiffen and move from time to time. It started to rain harder, so he decided to stop until it let up. A giant tree stood off to his left and he guided the horse under it. He slid from the saddle holding Sunny, and then put her down. She walked over and sat on the ground under the big tree, huddling there and not saying a word. Isaiah followed behind her and, almost falling from exhaustion, sat down. He put his arm around his daughter and pulled her against him, also not saying anything. No words seemed to be needed now.

Jonah loosened the saddle on the horses, took his rifle, and sat down beside them. "We may as well rest while it's raining so hard. It should let up in a while."

They settled down on the ground with their heads resting on the big roots of the trees. The hoods of their slickers covered their faces. Sunny's father continued to hold her against him, keeping her warm and safe. They soon feel asleep. Jonah's rifle was tucked beneath one leg to keep it dry and in easy reach. He knew they were both exhausted. His thoughts would not let him sleep. The kid had three brothers, and he wondered where they were and what they would do if they found him or his horse. His mind kept replaying all the tortured images of what probably happened to Sunny. She seemed so dejected, and

73

he just didn't know what to do for her. Men were worthless when it came to these kinds of things.

Jonah catnapped while it rained. It let up after an hour or so, but they were still sleeping. He decided to let them rest a little longer. Jonah still had most of the night to get her home. He wanted her safe from wagging tongues. If he got her home before daylight, everyone would think she was found down the trail a short way from home. After an hour of sleep, he woke them.

They rode the rest of the way home in sprinkling rain. It would rain harder for a while, and then let up, but the slickers kept them fairly dry and warm. When they rode into town, it was a few hours before dawn. The town was asleep, with no lights on. A few dogs barked from time to time. Jonah rode slowly through the dark early morning and turned down Francis Street to Sunny's house. He stopped Warrior in front of her door and slid from the saddle holding her.

"You're home, sweetheart," he said, as he looked into her eyes. The rain dripped from his hat, and he had it tipped over her head to protect her from the wet night.

"Thank you, Jonah, for rescuing me," she said as she looked into his eyes. She ran her hand into his hair and touched her lips to his. His knees almost buckled when she kissed him deeply and long. Emotions ran through him, deep and powerful. He had never felt so complete in his whole stinking life. Jonah had walked around all his life frozen and she had thawed him out. He stung from the melt, never being the same again. She slowly brought her lips from him and looked at him with shining blue eyes. "Oh, Jonah!" she said, as she put her arms around his neck. With her still in his arms, he turned with her and walked up to the door as it was jerked open by her mother. Bess let out a cry and reached for her. He knew Sunny's mother hadn't slept all night. She went into her mother's arms, and Bess took her inside the house.

"Thank you, my friend, for bringing my daughter home. The young deputy would never have found her, and it's no telling what else that kid would have done to her," Isaiah said, gratefully.

"No need to thank me. I don't think anybody could have stopped me from finding her."

"All the same, I'm grateful," he said as he shook his hand. Jonah tipped his hat, picked up Chico's reins, mounted his horse and rode slowly down the street. He looked back for a moment, knowing the people inside would comfort each other.

♥

Chapter 10

Jonah went into the smithy after taking care of the horses. Starting a fire and putting some coffee on helped him to wait until Clay opened his office. He could have gone to his friend's house, but didn't want to wake him. Jonah took a seat on the nail keg and leaned back against the wall. His body was tired, but his mind wasn't. He could still feel her warm lips. She was probably just thankful, but he certainly had more in his heart than that. He wanted to carry her home with him and take care of her. He encountered the kid a couple of times before and knew he was big trouble, but never believed in his wildest dreams that he would ever do something like this. It was unreal how people treated each other. He wanted to kill him again, even though he was trying to swallow his guilt. Jonah knew it hadn't been his right to take the kid's life. He hadn't even thought it out that far, his rage had taken over.

Jonah didn't remember ever being so exhausted, but he knew most of it was emotional. Physically he had done much more than he had done today. After pouring himself a strong black cup of coffee there was nothing to do but wait.

He heard a dog bark and a door bang in the distance. People were starting to move. It was getting close to morning. Clay might be in his office by now so Jonah got up and wandered across the street in the drizzling rain. The street was muddy so he sloshed his way through, just as it was turning daylight. He was thankful that they had brought Sunny home in the dark, before people started stirring.

Jonah stepped inside the door as Clay was stuffing wood into the stove to build his fire. He turned to see who came in, straightening up he looked at his friend.

"I guess you're here about Sunny. I got home late last night. Marie told me about it, but there wasn't anything I could do in the middle of the night. Is there anything new to add?" he asked, looking hopeful.

"Finish what you're doing, and we will talk."

Jonah told him what happened, ending with the fact that she was home before daylight.

"Where did you find her?"

"In the hills, in an old lean-to."

"Did you find the kid?"

"Yeah! I killed him."

Clay snapped to alert in his chair, looking at Jonah, clearly startled by what he said.

"You killed him? How?"

"I found the skunk outside. I knew I was too late, and when he admitted it, I challenged him to a gunfight, letting him know he had no choice."

"Did he draw?"

"Yeah!"

"Where did you bury him?"

"I didn't. I left him for the buzzards," Jonah admitted hatefully, settling back in his chair across from his friend.

"I know he deserved that, but I probably need to go bring him in to the undertaker and notify somebody, don't you think?" Jonah shrugged his shoulders to let Clay know he didn't really care.

"I didn't see where young deputy Hayden has made it back." Jonah questioned with sarcasm.

"Aw, hell, He's probably in Boston by now, following every track between here and there."

"Think he will ever learn and be any use to you?"

"If mistakes teach you anything, he will be a real slick dude someday."

"Am I in any kind of trouble over this?" Jonah asked, pushing his wet hat back.

"I don't see any problem. It was a gunfight. We will probably have to face his brothers sometime, but we will take it as it comes," he said, as he sat on the side of his desk, blowing on his hot coffee. He looked at Jonah. He hadn't seen his friend look so troubled.

"How's Sunny?"

"She has a lot to go through. As far as you know, I got there in time to stop any mischief that he might have had on his mind."

"He's dead now. No need to bring details to anyone," he replied as he tipped his head to his friend.

"I had better get to work before Simon opens and wonders where I am."

"I will ride up and bring his body back. Can I borrow a packhorse?"

"I will go with you."

"Appreciate it. See you shortly."

They found the kid right where Jonah had left him, with his gun laying on the ground beside him. They wrapped him in a blanket and put him on the packhorse. Clay poked around the area. He knew Jonah was telling him the truth, but he had his job to do, no matter what. He concluded by what he could find that everything looked like it happened the way Jonah said.

"No matter how you hate a fellow, killing him kinda tears your guts up," Jonah remarked as he laid his arms across his horse's saddle, watching Clay.

"Is it your first?" Clay asked as he stopped looking around and stood up.

"Yeah! I have come close a few times, but I always figured if I did the deed, I would hang for it. Being a breed would have made me in the wrong," he said as he looked off into space. "I figured it would happen before now, but somehow things always worked out right."

"Probably because you can look as mean as a rattlesnake, and that scares the crap outta them, and they give it a second thought." Clay surmised in jest.

"I'm not sorry I killed him. I would do it again for her but there's still that guilt that settles in your innards."

"Do you think Sunny will get over this any time soon?"

"I just don't know. Women are different from men. I feel at a loss sometimes when it comes to her. I don't even know if I handled things right," Jonah said as he took the reins from around the saddle horn."

"You will do right just as long as you're there to comfort her. Women are stronger than men give them credit for." Clay stated as he tied the packhorse to his saddle.

They mounted their horses and headed back to town. Jonah hoped he wouldn't need to ride this trail again.

Clay had already taken the kid to the undertaker and had gone about his business when the young deputy and his posse finally made it in.

"Clay, did you hear what happened?" the young deputy asked as he rushed into the sheriff's office. "We lost the tracks somewhere and when we tried to backtrack there were so many hoof-prints that we didn't know which ones were which. What do we do now?" he asked.

"She's already back, deputy. Jonah and Isaiah found her last night and brought her home."

"Where did they find her?"

"Somewhere in the hills. Jonah had a gunfight with the kid that took her and brought her home safe and sound."

Burning with resentment, Hayden just stepped back and said, "I'm glad."

Jonah hadn't seen Sunny since he brought her home. Isaiah dropped by to talk to him and told him she was doing well enough. That didn't set his mind at ease. He worried about her. Often noticing Sunny's mother going to the post office and around town, he knew she wasn't up to it yet. It had only been a week, and didn't expect her to be back to normal this soon. Jonah wanted to help her, but he didn't know what to do.

When the horse had come home riderless, the kid's brothers had gone to search for him. They came into town and claimed the body. They sadly told Clay they weren't surprised but he was their brother just the same. They held no animosity against anyone and just took him home.

Jonah sent Simon home to pick them up some lunch, and was having a cup of half warm coffee when Sunny walked in. She moved into the dark corner of the room. He went to her.

"How are you?" Jonah asked anxiously as he lifted her chin up to look at her.

Raising her eyes, she shook her head slowly from side to side, her blue eyes sad and troubled.

"Tell me," he said compassionately drawing her into his arms. She snuggled against his chest and let Jonah hold her. She sighed and put her arms around him.

"I have dreams every time I go to sleep about him hurting me all over again. I don't want Mama and Papa to think I'm having so much trouble; they would worry. I wash and wash but I can't get clean," she answered miserably, as tears welled up in her eyes and her voice shook with emotion.

"Oh sweetheart, you're clean. This was not anything you did. I'm sure your Mama and Papa don't expect you to get over everything this fast."

"They think I should go downtown like always so people won't wonder what's wrong with me. They might start adding things up if I'm not acting right."

"They are just trying to protect you. Just take a baby step at a time. The first time will be the worst. Start out by just going to the General Store with your mom. See if you can handle that before you try the next thing. They don't know what happened. They can only guess. Would you like to walk over to the General Store with me for the first time," he asked, concerned.

"No, I will try to walk down the boardwalk, go home, and act as normal as possible. Then Mama and I will go to the store together tomorrow."

"You can do it," he stated, smoothing the side of her face with his hand. "Don't let this control your life."

Tears welled in her eyes. "I can't help it. I wish the dreams would go away. I don't ever want to go to sleep. I still hate him, Jonah. I didn't know I was capable of it. Papa says to pray for help so that I can eventually forgive him. In my mind, I'm so glad he's dead I know that isn't how I should feel. I have always believed in forgiveness."

"Someday you will get your life back, but for now, try rolling up a quilt like a body lying beside you. Pretend it's your mother or someone you love, and lay against it during the nights. Make it your comforter. I used to do that when I was a kid, and it helped."

"Who did you pretend it was?" she asked, compassionately.

"I made it my mother."

"I will do that Jonah. If you made it through when you were little, I can too."

"That's my girl! If I can ever do anything, you just ask," he said tenderly.

"Jonah, do you think of me as a ruined woman now?" she asked miserably.

"No. Never. Those kinds of people can't take anything of value from you if you don't let them. I know you don't feel that way right now, but in time you'll be able to. To me, you're still the beautiful young woman I know. He couldn't change that."

"Thank you Jonah."

"Sweetheart, none of this was your fault. None of it! He stole from you. He was the lowest kind of snake in the grass."

They walked across the street together, appearing normal, as always. When she got to the boardwalk he said goodbye to her and watched as she made her way home.

That night, she rolled up a quilt like Jonah advised, snuggling against it. Instead of visualizing her mother as the comforter, Sunny pretended it was Jonah with his arms around her, remembering the tenderness of his embrace when he found her. She ran it through her mind, again and again, until sleep came. It was the first night that nightmares didn't torment her. Sunny woke refreshed. She knew she still didn't want to face anyone. That unwelcome chore had to be overcome to heal herself. With God's help, she knew it would be possible. She'd always trusted people, but that was in the past. Sunny had learned a brand new lesson; there was the dark side of humanity, and she would be aware from now on.

Sunny began the day by walking the way she had before her traumatic incident, following her normal route. It was hard but she gritted her teeth and made herself do it. She started for a short time period, and then added a little more time each day. She began to feel like visiting Molly, Doc, and the General Store and always stopped by to see Jonah and Simon, relaxing more there.

One morning she awoke from a terrible dream, but not the one that had recently been plaguing her. It was early, not yet dawn. Sunny jumped from her bed, dressed and slipped from the house. She was sure that Jonah would be open by now. Seeing him was imperative. She walked into the smithy and found him building a fire. He stopped when he saw her, and went to her.

"What's the matter," he asked, putting his hands on her arms.

"I woke from a horrible dream, one that could be true. I dreamt I was going to have his baby. Oh, Jonah I can't be. I would hate that child. What if I am?"

"Is there any reason why you think that could be true?"

"Not yet. Maybe... later... I could know" she stammered.

"Don't get worried about it yet. You probably just thought of the possibility, and it came out in your dreams."

"I would hate that baby Jonah."

"No, no you wouldn't," he said as he laid his hands on her shoulders. "It's not an innocent baby's fault. Anybody can make a baby. I know; I had one no-account father. I didn't have anything to do with their lives, but I got blamed. You would love it, because it would be yours and you'd forget how he came to be. I have faith in you Sunshine."

"You make me ashamed of my thoughts," she said softly, laying her head against his chest.

"You have every right! Don't be scared. We will cross every problem when they arise, okay?" he said, pulling her into his arms.

"I'm sorry I'm such a big baby," she replied.

"You have that right too. You need to go home now so nobody catches you here this early. People will be spreading other stories. I will follow behind you close enough to make sure you're okay."

Jonah followed behind her half a block or so until she entered her house.

♥

Chapter 11
1860

The Patee House, the finest hotel west of the Mississippi, was St. Joseph's best. All the activity seemed to be there lately. The Pony Express office and the Union Army office were there, and had been since the border wars had started. Blue uniforms flowed in and out of the hotel constantly. Camps set up in the hills where the roads led into town.

Jonah didn't think it looked too good. The border wars were escalating farther south at a fast pace. November was election time and Jonah knew, depending on who was elected, how things would happen. He had a gut feeling that Lincoln was going to win, and hell on earth would be the result. On the other hand, things would just drag out if he wasn't elected. Jonah knew these divided ideas over slavery weren't going away. He breathed in the springtime air, thinking it smelled good, like freedom that may be short lived.

He wished he knew how Sunny was doing. She seemed to make it out every few days, but he only saw her at a distance with her mom or Molly Allred, always giving him a wave. He knew she was trying to get back to normal. It had been awhile since he'd had a chance to talk to her, and he missed that. Deciding to stretch his legs, he walked down the street to see if he could find Clay. His friend was coming out of the hotel just about the time he reached the front.

"Don't tell me you're hanging around the hotel now too," Jonah chuckled as he stepped up to Clay.

"No, but they are setting up a Union recruiting office in there now. There's not much doubt about the coming war as far as they are concerned," Clay explained, wrinkling his brow.

"They are kinda getting a jump on things aren't they?"

"They say no. Quantrill is on the rise. Everybody is just sittin' on their thumbs until November, waitin' to see what they are sure is going to happen. They don't want to be sittin' high and dry, they tell me."

"Here I was just enjoying the nice spring day. This sure put a damper on it."

"Sorry buddy, it didn't exactly make my day either," Clay stated, as he slapped his friend on the shoulder.

"I guess I will finish my walk while I still can." Jonah declared.

"Can you wait a minute? I need to talk to you."

"Sure, what about?"

"I had to fire Hayden. I found out he was involved in a little movement going on to support the Confederacy. He can believe what he wants in his heart, but as a lawman he has to be neutral. I have my own beliefs; but I can't have them in my office."

"Too bad they are not all as honest as you are, my friend," Jonah answered, with the deepest respect.

"The problem is," he said as he tipped his hat back and shook his head, "I'm in no position to control anything he does anymore. I think he would have caused you a lot more problems over Sunny if I hadn't kicked his tail around over it a few times. So be careful, Jonah."

"You think he will try to shoot me in the back or something?"

"Naw. I think his words are going to be the problem."

"You're telling me to keep away from Sunny?"

"No buddy. I'm just saying be careful. Who knows? He didn't exactly keep his mouth closed before, so it might get worse."

After Jonah left and walked on down the street a bit, he found a boy giving away some mix breed puppies. Brat had been a mutt, but turned out to be great for Simon. The dog had been a real anchor in Simon's life during a hard time. He decided to get one for Sunny, and hoped this puppy would help her. He picked out a little feisty black and white spotted one that was a little hairier than the others. Maybe the little guy would take some of Sunny's sadness away. It killed him to see the hurt in her eyes.

Clay's words made him stop and think. He wasn't going to give the young deputy anything to cause that family any problems. He could handle what came his way, but he wasn't willing to be the cause of their grief.

After supper Simon and he showed up at Sunny's house with the puppy. She was so excited over it. The Markley's invited him to stay and have some apple pie. After trying a lot of names on her new pet, Sunny finally decided on Patches because of a spot on his back that almost looked like a quilt patch. Isaiah thanked Jonah for the dog. He admitted that a dog hadn't even crossed his mind. He knew Isaiah and Bess were worried about her but was happy she was making progress.

Jonah made her a little halter of sorts, with a lead rope so she could walk with her new pet without having to carry him or chase him down. Soon she was bringing her puppy along every time she when to town. She stopped by the smithy showing off the new pet and visited for awhile.

She confided to Jonah that she wasn't going to have a child. Her fears about that turned to relief. Still having bad dreams from time to time, but between the rolled up quilt, and her lively little Patches, she was on the way to handling them a little better. When Sunny took the puppy out at night, she was terrified that someone was lurking about. She knew she had to get over her worries, but sometimes they were bigger than she could handle.

Sunny talked to Jonah whenever she was scared, and he listened to her fears, assuring her that the culprit was gone forever. He told her that as a kid he often wished he had a friend or even an old granny just to have someone to talk to. After a time he invented one to help him get through his miserable childhood. Sunny was glad that he took the time to listen to her. She thought he was better than an invisible friend.

Jonah knew that if someone noticed her at his place alone things could get bad for her, especially if that person was the previous young deputy. Clay was right. Hayden's words would do more damage than anything. Everyone believed that he had found her before anything happened. Jonah didn't want stories about her visiting him at the smithy alone. He worried about it constantly, but she needed to talk, so he didn't say anything to her.

Sunny hadn't been to see Molly in a while, so she took Patches and went to visit her. They had such a nice time, catching up. Molly told her that she was going to have a baby. Sunny was very happy for her.

Sunny wanted to tell Molly what really happened, but she knew the less folks knew the better. People had quit asking her about her ride of terror. It seemed to be old news since she had gotten rescued so quickly; nobody seemed to think it was much of a dilemma. She still went about her daily routine, and it was getting easier but sometimes any kind of noise would cause her to panic. One day a stranger had been riding down the street and he looked at her. Sunny had stopped and backed up against the wall, her heart was beating so fast, and it took awhile to regain control. She hated being scared.

*   *

May turned into June and Sunny began to feel better. Time was helping, even though she still had nightmares. She went back to work for Doc, and that took her mind off of her problems, but at night she always woke up scared and wanting Jonah. The puppy and the quilt helped, but it wasn't the same. She loved Jonah desperately and wondered how he felt about her. Did he care, even a little? He was so busy right now that she hated to bother him. She hadn't seen him in days, except from a distance. It seemed like people were always at his place wanting some farm equipment fixed or their horses shod. Every time she stopped by he had work to do, or customers to help.

She knew he opened early, and made his coffee there. It was always easier to go see him then. She walked in while he was setting things up for work.

"Good morning, Sunshine," he said, looking at her to see if she was alright."

"You have been so busy every time I drop by that I haven't bothered you. I just wanted to see you for a few minutes."

"Want some coffee?"

"No," she said as she shook her head. "I want you to hold me Jonah, please."

He walked over and took her in his arms.

"Is something the matter?" he asked, concerned.

"Just that I love you Jonah," she stated, burying her face in his chest. His arms moved from around her, up to her shoulders and pulled her back from him, tipping her face up. "No, Sweetheart you are just feeling close to me because I rescued you and we share a secret that you can talk to me about."

"I felt this way before anything ever happened. I have loved you for a long time," she snapped, her eyes flashing with anger. "Do you think that I'm a child, and don't know what I feel."

"No, I don't think you're a child, but you have been through a lot."

"Do you think I would have loved anybody that rescued me?"

"No, don't be silly… It's just that…"
She cut him off in mid-sentence, and pulled out of his arms. "It's just that you don't feel the same. Be honest. I didn't expect you to tell me that you loved me back unless you really felt it."

"It isn't that, it's just…"

Again she cut him off in the middle of his words. "Then you do love me?" she asked defiantly.

"Will you let me talk?"

"No, just tell me the truth, do you or don't you? That's not hard to answer." She said, folding her arms across her chest.

"Listen to me for a minute…"

"No! answer me," she shouted.

"Okay, I do love you. Is that what you wanted to hear?" he said, with a half-whisper.

"Yes," she said, as she walked back into his arms, kissing him, like she had wanted to for so long. He could not push her away. He kissed her with all the feelings that had been stored away in his heart. He had loved her for such a long time, and he couldn't tear his lips from her, or his arms, or his heart. Through all the emotion something niggled in the back of his brain. He knew what it was. It was what he had always known, that he could not have her. He gently pushed her from his arms and looked down into her eyes. It would kill him to tell her, for she was the one thing in life that he really wanted.

"You know I can never marry you. People would make your life miserable."

"It's not because...?" she asked, not finishing her sentence, looking down to avoid his eyes.

He grabbed her by the shoulders, looking at her with indignation. "You know better than that. That has nothing to do with any of this. I'm not good enough for you, I am half Indian, I was raised by the worst people imaginable, and I will not make your life miserable. People would call you names and despise you. Your life would not be the same. I will not have anything to do with that."

"I don't care what people think. I love you. The only thing stopping me is a danger to your life."

"I can take care of myself. Don't you worry about me? Think about yourself."

"Does that mean that you will marry me?"

"No, I can't ever marry you."

"Maybe we could get married. People like you, Jonah. Most people don't think of you as a half-breed. It might be different if we got married, rather than just seeing each other."

Jonah took her by the shoulders. "No, Sweetheart, it wouldn't work."

"You don't know that for sure. Let's talk to Doc and see what he thinks."

"No Sunny, I will never marry you. Do you understand? Never," he said, holding her firmly by the shoulders. Tears rolled down her cheeks as she looked into his eyes, and saw his misery too.

"Okay, I understand," she whispered, as she backed away from him. "You just remember that I love you and I always will. I have never loved a man before. I looked for the right one for years, and nobody ever stole my heart until I met you. I may marry someday, but you will have to know that he was second choice. Remember," she said, wiping her eyes as tears streamed down her cheeks. "I will always wish I could have married you."

"Me too," he said, softly.

"Maybe one of these days things will be different."

"I hope so Sweetheart, but it probably won't be in our lifetime. You have to make a life without me. But I will never be sorry I knew you. Men look for gold, but my gold was in you Sunshine. You're the best thing that ever happened to me."

With tears streaming down her face she walked over and threw her arms around his neck. He buried his face into her shoulder as he held her tight.

"Go home now," he said, with effort for his throat was burning and his own eyes were about to betray him.
She gently kissed him then turned and left. He walked to the door and watched her walk down the street as daylight started to move in, and when she turned out of sight, he turned around and kicked the nail keg across the floor.

♥

Chapter 12

Jonah hadn't slept well for a week, not since Sunny had told him that she loved him. He would talk himself into thinking it could work out, and then would regain his senses and know that it never could. His worst nightmare would be to look into her eyes and see that she no longer cared. That would kill him. He was still stinging with pain from feelings that she brought to life and spent half the night on the porch looking at the stars.

Was Sunny's God really up there? He never saw any signs of Him when he was a kid. Where was He then? Where was He now? Was Jonah missing something? Could this mighty God make things different? He felt like his life had never meant anything to anybody. Then this God played a big trick on him, sending a beautiful lady to him, one he could only dream about. What a joke!

Jonah was tied in knots wanting and knowing he couldn't have her and was angry because nothing could be changed. He had always accepted whatever was in his life and had learned to live with it. But Sunny, that was something he couldn't change and was too dangerous to even try. He wouldn't risk her life, or even her way of life.

The yearning in him would probably never go away. He hadn't seen her in over a week and he felt deprived, but he had to let her decide what to do with her life. He went back to bed, but knew sleep wasn't going to come easily.

"Hey Jonah, are you busy?"

"Not really, Doc. What do you need?" he asked, as Doc walked up to him.

"Will you grab your hammer and come over to my office for a minute? I need something fixed."

"What is it?"

"Just grab your hammer and come along and I'll show you."

Jonah picked up his hammer and followed Doc down the street to his office. They walked inside.

"Okay, what's the problem?" he asked, looking around.

Doc walked over and took the hammer from his hand. "Someone is waiting for you in my parlor. Go on back there. Don't keep her waiting."

Jonah didn't have to be told who it was, so he walked back to Doc's living quarters. Sunny looked up as Jonah entered. Her eyes looked miserable.

"I asked Doc to bring you here, so I could say goodbye to you privately," she said, as her chin quivered, holding back the tears.

"Goodbye? Where are you going?" he asked, as he took her hands in his.

"I'm going back to Virginia to live with my brother for a while. I don't see what else I can do," she explained as tears streamed down her face. "I need to be away from here so I can get back to being myself again. That's only part of it. I can't be with you, and I can't stay away from you. I know I'll only cause you problems if I stay here. My father heard Hayden and some of his friends talking in front of the hotel the other day. They're saying bad things about you. Please be careful Jonah. He is up to no good."

"Don't you worry about Hayden or anyone else, I can handle them."

Sunny slowly put her arms around him trying to hold back the tears and laid her head on his shoulder. Jonah gathered her into his arms.

"But I do worry about you. I love you. I need to be away from everything going on in my life so that I can work things out. My brother has always been my best friend. I'm hoping that he can give me a new way to look at myself."

"That probably would be the best thing for you then." Jonah commented, his heart sinking. He didn't know if he could handle never seeing her again.

"I need to trust in the Lord and right now I'm feeling sorry for myself. I need to be more like Joseph. Do you know the story of Joseph in the Bible, Jonah?"

"No, I don't know much about the Bible." he answered, looking at her.

"Come over here. I have something for you," she replied, as she walked to the couch and picked up a Bible. She sat down and Jonah walked over and settled down beside her. She turned to him, placing the Bible in his hands. "I'm giving this to you. While I'm gone, I want you to read it so you'll know who God is, and the things he promises. Joseph was a young man who trusted in God. It was twelve years before the Lord brought him out of his bondage, but he never quit believing. God's promises came through for him, but in God's time, not in Joseph's. I'm going to need that kind of trust. I know there has to be a way we can be together, and He's going to show me how. A terrible thing happened to me, and I'm going to heal. In the meantime, wait on me Jonah. If you love me, don't marry someone else while I'm gone. Please," she begged, as she dropped her face into her hands and began to sob. Jonah pulled her into his arms. Pretending not to want her was no longer going to work. He stroked her back and buried his face in her hair as she cried.

"I won't ever marry anyone else. You're the only woman in the world for me. I love you Sweetheart," he proclaimed softly.

"Promise?"

"Promise," he replied. "We'll die trying to find a way to be together," he lied, knowing there would never be a way for them.

She lifted her face to him and took his hand in hers. "I'm leaving. I'll always love you Jonah. Please don't forget that. I'm not giving up. There's some way and some time that we can be together, and I am going to find it. Until then, the best thing I can do is get away from you until Hayden and anyone else like him who hates us for our feelings, can forget it. Don't ever quit loving me," she added.

"Quit loving you! The only way that would be possible is if I am six feet under."

"Kiss me, a kiss that will last for a long time," she asked, looking at him with emotion she didn't even try to hide. Jonah kissed her until he was drowning in sensation. How could he let her go, and how could he not? He had no faith that someday they could be together, but he would let her think it might work out. Maybe she would find someone, someday, and forget all about him. It killed him to think that, but he loved her enough to want the best for her. He just hoped he would see her again. He held her for a long time, and they said their goodbyes. The couple made their promises until Isaiah and Bess came to take her to the train station.

Jonah closed up his place early that day; the first time in fourteen years. No one noticed him walk into the hills and stand against a tree, looking below as a train moved smoothly over the tracks taking his life away.

If he thought he couldn't sleep before, he really couldn't now. He spent half his night out on the porch, tending his bleeding heart. For a man that hadn't felt much in his life, he was certainly making up for it now.

Jonah snapped at everybody. Was the whole world all at once irritating him to death?

One day Clay stopped in late in the day.

"I'm getting ready to close. What do you need?" Jonah snapped, as he put a tool back on the hook.

"You really are an old bear, aren't you? I heard tell you have turned into the town crab," Clay announced as he leaned against the door.

"I'm not in the mood for this. Spit it out, and get on your way," he replied, his eyes snapping with anger.

"Phew," Clay whistled. "I think you had better sit down son, and tell papa all about it."

Jonah jerked his hat off, threw it on the floor, and ran his hands through his hair in frustration. He walked over and sat down on the nail keg. Clay reached down and picked his hat up and handed it to him. Jonah sat there, running his hands around the brim, with his elbows resting on his knees.

"She told me she loved me. As bad as I wanted to marry her, how could I?

"So she left. What else could she do? Everybody has been telling her she can't have you."

"Clay, I love her. I couldn't marry her. I am a half-breed, no-account."

"Where in the world do you get these notions that you're a nobody? You're my best friend and I don't have no-account friends. Maybe she saw the fine man that I know."

"People around here don't have regards for Indians. You know that."

"Jonah, we all have different nationalities running in our veins. That's what America is, a melting pot of every race, religion and creed. I'm Irish. There was a time the Irish were as unwelcome as anyone. The Scots and Irish were only fit to send into Indian territory to do jobs that other people wouldn't risk their lives to do. You have never lived in an Indian camp, have never scalped anyone, and never even spoken the language. It's got to change one of these days. Most people here don't think of you as an Indian but those few that do are the problem."

"My old man used to call me a no-account half-breed."

"Well he wasn't worth shootin'! You're a good man, and Sunny loves you. Don't give up. Maybe this war that's brewing will change a few things."

"I got my doubts."

Jonah hadn't opened the Bible Sunny gave him. He picked it up from the dresser and carried it to the table and flipped it open to the first page. There she had written:

Jonah,
I love you with all my heart. Don't give up! Be faithful, and hold on. Read Joseph's story in Genesis 37. I will be in your arms to stay someday.
Sunny.

Jonah flipped the pages over until he came to the chapter and verse. He started to read the trials of a young man who had been hurt by the betrayal of his brothers. He read his story, amazed at the goodness and faith he held onto through the years. He had no hatred or animosity toward anyone who mistreated him. He kept his faith in God, day after day, holding onto to nothing but a dream that God had given him. Twelve years later the Pharaoh made Joseph the second in command over all of Egypt. He could had his brothers killed with a snap of his fingers, and nobody would have cared. Instead he saved them and brought them to Egypt with him. In God's timing, Joseph's answer came. His faith in God was well rewarded. Jonah closed the book, knowing that he was now interested in knowing more about Sunny's God. What made people so faithful to a God that didn't give them everything they wanted. Sunny kept right on believing, even after the things she had gone through. Why? He needed to know.

*   *

Sunny had been in Virginia for two months. She was not sad and depressed because of what the kid had done to her, but rather because she missed Jonah. She was sitting on the porch swing like she did most evenings with Patches. Her little puppy had grown a lot, and was a great comfort to her. Levi and Mary were wonderful, and she loved little Samuel, but her heart hurt.

"Mind company?" her brother asked.

"Of course not. Sit down." He crossed over and sat beside her, Patches moved into her lap. Levi moved the swing in a slow motion. Neither said a word for a minute, just watching the sunset.

"It's beautiful isn't it?" she commented.

"You want me to beat him up for you?" he asked looking at her.

"No! He's a good person. You would really like him"

"So you have told me, but it's hard to see my little sister so miserable. I didn't think I would ever see the day when anything got you down. You have always been so full of life."

"It's been hard the last few months," she replied, as she rubbed Patches.

He put his arms around her shoulders and pulled her against him. "It will get better. The valleys are tough, but they don't last forever. Would you like to help out at my office? You might have more to do and get your mind off of things. You have never been one to sit around."

"Are you creating a job for me?"

"Kind of but my assistant has a lot to do, and I know he would appreciate the help."

"You must be a good lawyer if you're that busy."

"I don't do much as a lawyer. Running Grandfather's business, I have to know the law."

"Thanks, but I would rather help out at the hospital. I have just been putting it off. I have to get up and go again soon, I know."

"I think that would help you more than anything."

"I know you're right. I am just feeling sorry for myself."

"Do you love him that much?" Levi asked, looking at his sister with concern.

"I do. Someday, someway, I am going to figure out a way for us," she stated with determination.

"I don't doubt that one bit. That sounds more like my scrappy little sister," he said smiling.

She started working at the hospital with some of the same people she had worked with before she left Virginia to go to Missouri. It helped to keep her mind occupied during the day, but the nights were hard. Her mind would not let her rest. Sunny thought of Jonah and ached for the sight of him. Since her thoughts were always on Jonah, her horrifying experience with the kid took up less space. She thought she would never get past it, but her fear of something like that happening again began to fade.

Sunny walked around her old neighborhood, met some of her former friends, and began to feel like herself again. She prayed that God would take her hate away, and soon realized that it was no longer a constant companion in her soul. She was healing, and knew she would be well in time, but would never quit loving Jonah. Sunny decided that love was much harder to banish than hate.

♥

Chapter 13

Clay noticed that there was a real sadness about Jonah. He had never seen his friend look like that before, and he knew what the problem was. He walked into the smithy where Jonah was working the forge, just finishing up a wheel repair.

"Busy?" he asked.

"Naw, just fixin' a wagon wheel," he said as he propped it against the wall and joined Clay on the nail kegs.

"What are you up to?"

"Just dropped by to see if you were still kickin'."

"I'm still kickin'," he said as he took his hat off and ran his hands through his hair in frustration.

"Have you heard from Sunny?"

"No, and I worry about her constantly. Isaiah doesn't say a thing about how she's doing."

"Do you expect him to, if you don't ask?" Clay asked, looking at him hard.

"I thought he might, hoped he would. Isaiah gives Simon goodies to bring home that Mrs. Markley makes. He never says a thing about her."

"He probably doesn't know what to say to you. He can't tell you she's doing great. That might make you think she's already forgotten you. He can't tell you she's miserable. That might make you worry, so what is he supposed to tell you?"

"That she's safe, and sends her love."

"Ask him the next time you see him. You have that right, Jonah."

"How's Marie coming along with the baby?"

"Getting as big as a barn and as cute as a button. The girls are excited, hoping they get a baby brother.

"I'll bet you a cigar that it's a boy." Jonah said.

"I'll bet you that same cigar that Sunny is right, and she will figure out a way for you two. It's too right to be wrong."

Jonah just finished looking over the horses to see which ones needed shoes, or if any needed tending from cuts, scrapes or diseases. He walked up to Gypsy. She would always be Sunny's horse. A man had wanted to buy her at one point and offered a very good price, but he wouldn't sell her. If Sunny never came back, he doubted if he would ever get rid of her. Jonah rubbed the horse's well-shaped head, then ran his hands down her back, and checked her legs and feet.

"You're in great shape, Lady. Do you miss her too?" he asked, softly.

Gypsy whinnied as if she knew what he said. Jonah would never rid his mind of the memories. How many times she stood on the railing of the fence rubbing Gypsy's head with that smile, her teasing manner, and open friendliness that she extended to every person she knew. She took extra care of Simon, making him feel special. Most of all, Jonah would never forget her telling him how much she loved him. He, a half–breed, a nobody in this world, and Sunny loved him. She had choices and she picked him. Why?

Maybe Clay was right, Maybe Sunny was right. It isn't what people have or who they belong to. It comes down to who you are and what you believe. Maybe not even that. Why do men love one special woman, and why does that same woman love that man back. Maybe it is like Sunny says that God planned it for us. If God planned it for us, why can't it work out? Sunny says we need to be patient, that God has his own reasons and his own timing.

"If I believe that, then I'm going to believe that we will find a way someday too, and I will see her again. I don't believe I can live my lifetime unless I hold on to that." Jonah said out loud with only Gypsy close enough to hear.

Sunny walked home from work on Friday afternoon. She strolled along leisurely seeing the new fallen leaves jumping in the breeze. It helped her to work at the hospital, but she still missed St. Jo, her family, friends, and Jonah most of all. As she walked up to the house Patches met her wagging his tail and asking for affection. Sunny sat on the porch petting him. She heard little Samuel giggling and knew Mary was playing with him. She was such a good wife and mother. As Sunny entered the house, Mary was blowing kisses on his belly, and he would erupt into a fit of giggling. Sunny couldn't help but smile. Mary looked up as she came in. "You got to leave early today?" she questioned, as Samuel crawled from her lap and toddled over to his aunt. Sunny picked him up and hugged him. His two front teeth shone in a big grin. Patches started barking and running around Sunny's feet. He loved the baby as much as anyone.

"What is my little guy up to today?" she asked, kissing him on the neck.

"He runs me ragged sometime. He has more energy than two I think," Mary said, beaming at her son.

"You want me to play with him for a while."

"If you want and I will start supper. I hope he gets tired early tonight."

Sunny took him outside so he and Patches could play until suppertime.

Sunny did the dishes after supper. Mary was upstairs getting Samuel ready for bed and She had just finished, when Levi came in. "You're still not happy, Sun. It's been months, and hard as you try you don't have that cheerful disposition that you've had all your life," he said looking at her with concern.

"How would you feel if you had to leave Mary, not knowing if you would ever get to see her again?" she asked, as she took a seat at the table.

"I admit it would be hard."

"Don't worry about me. I am doing fine except I miss Jonah. That takes up a lot of my thoughts. I know you would like to help me, but it's something I have to work out by myself," she said as she patted his hand.

Sunny smiled, remembering how many times her big brother had given in and done something for her that she had pestered him about. He was so much like their father, tall, slim, and full of compassion for other people. Their grandfather, Arnold Snead, thought there was no one like his only grandson. He sent him to college to be a lawyer to help out in his shipping business, but Levi wanted to help people, not swindle them. It only deepened his grandfather's love and respect for him.

"Levi, do you think there is any way a white girl and a half-breed could live together peacefully."

"Move to an Indian camp," he stated, smiling.

"That might be our only answer," she replied as she chuckled, thinking about them living in a teepee.

"Do you write to him?

"No, I've been afraid it would make it harder," she said.

"Sis, you can put your feelings toward each other in a letter. Mary and I used to live through our letters when I was at college. I think we fell more and more in love. Sometimes people can pour their hearts out on paper, even more so than sitting side by side.

That evening before going to bed, she wrote her first letter to Jonah.

Dear Jonah,

I miss you more and more each day. My brother told me letters were a comfort, and that is what I need. If I can't see, touch or hold you then a letter has to be the next best thing. I have told you before how much I love you, and that will never change. I remember everything about you, like your teasing smile, raising of one eyebrow when you question something, your concern for people you care about, how your arms feel around me, and your serious eyes when you look at me. All the bad things in my life disappear when I think about you.

I wish you were here. I would show you my childhood home, where I used to live. Virginia with so many trees, not unlike Missouri and a huge oak that stood out front of our house, where my papa made a swing.. I would get so wild, and swing so high that my father threatened to remove it. Down the road lived a little girl I used to play with. Her name was Betsy and she was as spoiled as I. We fought over everything, but we still were the best of friends. I ran into her last week. She is a beautiful lady and is newly married. I told her I was getting married soon, hoping for that to be the truth.

There's old Mrs. Harper, our biggest gossip. I thought she was old when I was young, but she told me she was seventy-one. She was only in her late fifties when I knew her. She has been a widow longer than I have been alive. No wonder she gossiped. She had no children and no family, so she had nothing better to do. I feel sorry for her now. I used to get so mad at her for telling on me every time I did something naughty.

There was a trail in the woods that led to a shallow place in the river where we used to swim. I was never allowed to go there when I was young without my brother. Of course being the naughty little girl that I was, Betsy and I would sneak down there. We got caught every time. It took me years to figure out my mama knew where I was most all the time. It is time to close for now, but remember I keep you with me always.

With all my love,

Sunny.

She almost felt like they had a long conversation when she sealed the letter to mail the next day.

♥

Chapter 14
1860

November 1860 brought the election of Abraham Lincoln as the president of the United States. He declared that the government could not endure permanently with half slave and half free states. The southern states were infuriated, and a month later South Carolina seceded from the Union. Jonah wondered where it would all end. It didn't look good. St. Jo was divided over the differences and sometimes fights would break out over the issue.

Simon told him that if war broke out he wanted to go and fight for his people's freedom. Jonah knew he would have to go with him. It scared him to death to think about Simon dying on a battlefield somewhere and he wasn't there to protect him.

Jonah received Sunny's letter and read it over and over. He saw her as a little girl when she described events in her childhood. He smiled over some of the things she had done and he saw how she had grown into such an extraordinary woman. He still didn't believe he deserved her, even if things did work out for them, which he still doubted. Jonah wrote her back, reluctantly telling her about his childhood, describing the worst because she deserved to know all about him. She answered understanding none of it was his fault, always adding how much she loved and missed him.

Mack and Molly became their outlet for sending and receiving their letters, for they wanted to keep it a secret. When he saw one of them come to his place, he anticipated getting another letter from Sunny. They lived through them and poured out their hearts onto paper, reading them over and over.

December brought a lonely Christmas. It also brought a lot of uncertain feelings to everybody. How would the new year start out with a different president bearing new ideas? It also brought the birth of Clay's baby boy, followed shortly by the birth of Mack and Molly's son. Jonah had a deep ache in his heart, wondering if he would ever share that joy with Sunny. No matter how often he had told himself it couldn't be, he still dreamed foolish dreams. For a smart man, he knew he was dumb enough to torture himself with these thoughts.

During a big snowstorm in February, Jonah walked into Clay's office on his way home, shaking the snow from his hat as he sat down in the chair across from Clay. "It's flat out putting the snowflakes down outside," Jonah said.

"I saw that. The older I get, the more I realize that I don't care much for winter," he chuckled as he leaned back in his chair.

"How's that baby son? I haven't seen him much lately?"

"He's different from the girls, or maybe I forgot, but he is one busy kid," Clay said, smiling proudly.

"Maybe he seems busier since you're an old man," Jonah said teasingly.

"Young enough to get him though," he laughed.

"What do you think about all the unrest since Lincoln has been elected?"

"I don't know, my friend. I hope if there is war, it won't last long, but I wonder."

"I talked Simon out of joining for awhile. I don't have any idea what else I can do to stop him," he said, pushing his hat back on his head.

"Not much you can do. He's sixteen, and if anyone has a cause he does. Mack Reeves is joining, so are a few other young men around here."

"Mack is joining?" Jonah asked in shock. "Why?"

"He says it's right. He doesn't believe in slavery, but he believes in Lincoln"

"What does Molly say?"

"She's hating it, but says she has to let him do what he thinks is right. He promised her he would wait until next year."

"How divided is our state?"

"Well the middle of the state leans toward pro-slavery. Lots are on the other side, especially the German population. The rest is split.

"It's a bad dream, Clay."

"I know."

Four more states had seceded from the union. It was growing into a bigger giant all the time. Men were recruited and in training, for there was no doubt that there would be war. The question was when.

Jonah didn't have many problems when he didn't feel emotions. That seemed so long ago. He felt too much now. The child he raised meant a lot to him. He wasn't just any kid.

Sunny! He never shook her from his mind. She had been gone for months now, and it hadn't gotten one ounce easier. Her letters kept him going, but it wasn't like seeing her. With the talk of war so close at hand, he was now worrying about her safety too.

* *

1861

On April 12th, 1861 at 4:30 a.m., under command of Pierre Beauregard, the rebels opened fire with fifty cannons on Ft. Sumter, South Carolina. The war had begun! Jonah wasn't sure what the outcome would be. The paper stated that the war wouldn't last three months, but Jonah didn't believe that. There was only about ten percent of Missouri that even owned slaves, but he knew a lot of men would fight. The border wars had been going on for years. Now that war was actually happening, there would be plenty of men involved.

There were many resources in St. Jo to make cannons and bullets, and there was communication with waterways and railroads.

In September a fort had been erected on top of Prospect Hill and named after Colonel Smith a Union officer, who had it built. By mid-August the Confederacy was on its way to gaining control of Missouri. They would want to control St. Joseph because it was the epicenter for communication and transportation. It had the railroad system, the Pony Express, a steamboat port, and a telegraph center. Colonel Smith stood ready with 2,500 troops and twelve cannons. They could see for miles around the town.

Later in the month, guerillas sabotaged the railroad bridge over the river leading into town. The train fell into the river killing seventeen passengers. Soon thereafter, Union troops were everywhere to protect the communication and transportation from the rebels.

1862

January came too soon and Molly had gone with Mack to the train when he had to leave. She clung to him tearfully. Jonah tagged along with them to see Mack off. He walked Molly back home then went to see Clay.

"What are you up to?" Clay asked, as he leaned back in his chair.

"I went to the train with Molly to see Mack off. She cried her eyes out."

"A lot of wives are doing that right now," he said, shaking his head in sorrow.

"I think I have to go with Simon."

"Are you considering it?"

"Clay, I raised that boy for a lot of years. It's tearing me apart to think I won't be there," Jonah answered, removing his hat in frustration, and slapping it against his knee.

"Everybody has to make their own choice about this war. I don't think anybody will be able to be completely neutral," Clay said, discouraged.

"There is no way that I think slavery is right, but most of the South has been raised with it so I don't think they really understand. They need to be under authority of some tyrant for a while to understand it," Jonah said, emphatically.

107

"Some of the boys who are fighting for the Confederacy have never owned a slave or even been around any. They think they're fighting for a good cause, I'm sure!"

"Quantrill and his men are still trying to wipe out anyone they know is with the North. I'm glad Sunny's not here. If all the men go to war who's going to protect their women?" Jonah questioned.

Ft. Smith on the hill is the best we have. If the boarder renegades all got together it would take a whole cavalry to stop them.

There are about three hundred of those men, and we have a little less than four-hundred men in a cavalry.

"Thanks for making me feel better."

"Not much to feel good about, for sure. The government has already declared them outlaws, but who's going to stop them, except a whole regiment of soldiers."

"Who's going to help you if St. Jo gets invaded by the Confederate army?" Jonah asked, looking at his friend solemnly.

"There are a lot of Union soldiers in Missouri keeping the Confederate army out of here. That is their only job. They will have scouts, and hopefully will be here. I'm telling you Jonah, these renegades are going to get worse since the war has begun. They are already burning homes of people who they think are Union supporters. They wear blue coats, so the Union army will think they are one of theirs until they are right on top of them. They are the best riders in the world. They ride with both hands aiming blazing guns as they ride like the very devil. They don't fight like soldiers. They hide and attack when they have the advantage, and outnumber their prey. Quantrill and his men are riding with Price's army sometimes."

"I suppose they are killing children and raping women," Jonah said angrily.

"They have a twisted sense of right and wrong. They say they don't hurt white women. Of course there is no way they know about some of the riffraff that ride with them," Clay answered, shaking his head sadly.

"I heard that most of these things are happening farther south, on the Kansas line."

"Yes, but they are moving farther about. I heard most of their supporters are in the middle of the state. Our militia is trying to make sure they stay south, but how long is that going to last?"

The Union officers were in and out of St. Jo on a regular basis.

Jonah picked up the paper that he hadn't had time to read earlier. These days it seemed to be full of information.

"Confederacy maintains a toehold in southwest Missouri" the caption read.

It went on to tell how Captain Hiram Barstow sent a detachment of Union soldiers to Gainesville, but being outnumbered by the confederacy, they had lost the battle giving the Confederacy an advantage.

Jonah shook his head and frowned, "That doesn't sound too good," he commented.

"What doesn't sound good," Clay asked, as he walked over and stood behind Jonah, looking at the paper he was reading.

"This story in the paper, about losing to the rebels here in Missouri last week."

"I know. I read that too. We're going to have to do better than that if we expect to win."

"Do you think we have a prayer?

"I don't know. If you read on the next page it says President Lincoln has summoned a special session of Congress. He is issuing a proclamation for 75,000 militiamen. Sounds like he's worried too."

"I suppose so," Clay said, looking over Jonah's shoulder at the paper.

"More states seceded from the Union. It's like nobody's got a lick of brains."

"Men are joining everywhere on both sides. They act like it's some kind of a shindig instead of a war."

"President Lincoln issues a Proclamation of Blockade against Southern ports. This would limit the South from being well supplied against the war with the North." Jonah read. "Well, that might help some, I guess."

"Look at that Jonah. That ad has been in every issue of the paper for weeks now. They are having quite a time getting men to help build those telegraph lines for the Western Union. With the war they can't find the men to work.

"I would rather build lines between here and California than go to war. Seems like I don't have much choice though. Maybe a lot of people don't feel like they do either."

Jonah had a few things to do before he left. He felt flakes of snow coming down, and before he got to Clay's office it picked up the pace and really began to snow.

"Kinda wet, huh?" Clay said, as he watched Jonah step inside.

"Yeah, It's really snowing out there. Right now it looks like it means business."

"Well, it's January, That's a snow month."

"Got a minute?" Jonah asked, as he sat down.

"Sure do. What do you need?"

"I'm closing the blacksmith shop down while I'm gone, but I need someone to take care of the stables. Any suggestions?"

"You know, I was going to talk to you about that. A young fella came by my office the other day. He's a blacksmith and was looking for a job. He is staying with the Howard's right now. He tried his luck in the gold mines, and came away just as broke as when he arrived. Said he kept from starving to death by being a blacksmith and a hostler."

"Maybe I will take a ride out and talk to him. I would like someone to keep an eye on things. You could take care of the money, buy feed and pay his wages, until you know what kind of person he is."

"I can do that, my friend."

"I am dreading this Clay. This has become the only home I have ever known. I hate this crazy war." He looked around like he was fixing it in his mind. He pushed his hat back on his head.

"I know Jonah. I hate it too," Clay said, as the snow piled up on the window sill, making things look pretty and white, and covering the doom that lay ahead.

"You know as rough a life as I have lived; I have only killed one man."

"The kid?"

"Yeah, the kid. I hated him so much for what he did to Sunny that I couldn't let it go. Now I'm going to have to kill young boys Simon's age who haven't done anything."

"I know how tough you are, Jonah, but don't think you can save everyone. You save yourself," he said, as he leaned forward in his chair, so Jonah knew how serious he was about what he was saying. "I mean it. Don't give up just because things aren't what you want with Sunny. They never will be if you're dead. Thery're are always ways to work things out as long as you have breath left. You ever hear about the mouse that fell into a jug of milk. He didn't give up. He swam and swam, until he walked out on top of the butter he churned."

"You always have the answer to everything," Jonah chuckled, shaking his head at Clay's story.

Jonah took his hat off and ran his hands through his hair in frustration. He knocked the wet hat against his leg before putting it back on. "Will you do one more favor for me?" he asked, looking at his friend.

"Just name it?"

"If anything happens to me, I want everything I have to be split between Simon and Sunny. If anything happens to Simon, then give it all to Sunny. I wrote out a will."

He took out the papers and handed them to Clay. "I had it witnessed by Joseph. You can witness it too, okay? You make sure everything gets done right."

"I will, but you remember what I said. You take care of yourself. When are you leaving?"

"I talked Simon into waiting until March. I have things to take care of before I leave, and I hate freezing, I did plenty of that when I was a kid.

"I hate to see you go, my friend."

"I hate to go. Seems like my whole life has been doing things I didn't want to do. I suppose I can do this too."

After leaving Clay he decided to go talk to Isaiah. He walked up to their front door, kicking the snow out of the way. Bess ushered him into the kitchen and poured him a cup of coffee. Jonah hadn't seen her since Sunny left him.

"Would you like a slice of warm apple spice cake?" Bess asked as she went to get a plate and fork. Jonah didn't get sweets often enough, so he always took them when they were offered. She placed the cake in front of him. He ate it with more relish than usual. It was like he might never taste, smell, or feel the things he loved again.

"How have you been Jonah?" Bess asked as she joined him at the table with a cup of coffee for herself.

"As well as I can be, I guess."

"Isaiah has been over to the church, I think I just heard him come in." She got up and took his coat when he entered the house. After pouring himself some coffee, he sat at the kitchen table with Jonah.

"Hello Jonah," Isaiah said, as he blew on his hot coffee.

They talked awhile about the war. Then Jonah could stand it no longer, so he asked what was in his heart. "I want to ask about Sunny. Is she safe where she's at?"

"Yes, as safe as anyone can be right now," Isaiah said, as he wrinkled his brow with worry lines. "Virginia is going to be in the middle of it, that's for sure. I do wish she was home, but my son can care for as well as I can. She loves you Jonah. I hope the time comes when you can have each other without it being a big thing to anyone else."

"I'm sure you would like a half-breed for a son-in-law?" Jonah said, doubtfully.

"Do you think I wanted my daughter to marry a big time banker or some railroad baron? I want her to marry someone she loves, and she loves you. Ask my wife about love. She came from a prominent family. I wasn't good enough for her. They had forbidden her to marry me. We married anyway, and they disowned her. They really thought she would beg them to let her come back home. After seven years they finally realized that she wasn't going to. They made up with her. Levi was five years old then and Sunny was just a baby. Bess will tell you that she has no regrets. I know I am the lucky one, but she tells me she is just as lucky as I am. I have never been able to give my family all that they deserve. Bess's family sent Levi to law school. I let them, since I would never have been able to do that. But, we have been happy. My kids are good people. We have always loved each other, and the Lord has blessed us. We have had problems like anybody else, but that keeps us close to God. Sunny was brought into your life and you into hers for a reason. Sunny is like her mom. She loves for life," he said, smiling.

"I love her, you know."

"I know."

On his walk home he realized he should have grabbed on to Sunny like a drowning man when he had the chance. Who knows how long things might last. She might not have been able to stay with him, but oh, what memories he would have had of her. If nothing else good ever came into his life, and when he was nearing the end, just loving her would be enough. If he lived to be a hundred and never saw her again he would never lose her image, her feel, her scent. He had put her on like an extra layer of skin. She had invaded all of his senses, and brought him to life. But real life felt pain, and oh, how he was in pain. It was a worse pain than his childhood. He couldn't change his upbringing, and right now he couldn't change this.

Jonah met Ian Campbell, the man Clay told him about. He was shorter than Jonah, but fit, letting Jonah know that he was used to hard work. Ian Campbell was an

Irishman in his late twenties. He had the slightest brogue. Jonah liked his easy going, straight-forward manner. After talking to Ian, Jonah decided to let him run the whole business.

"Sounds like you know your way around a smithy. I'm leaving in about a week, so I will just hang around and watch you work for a few days. And introduce you to my horses," Jonah stated..

"I can tell you know horses. Each one has its own character," Ian said smiling.

"That they do. Just like people." Jonah agreed. "One little sorrel mare named Gypsy is special. She isn't to be rented or sold. She doesn't work for her keep. Just take her around for a stretch occasionally when you have time. Keep her in shape."

"Is she your personal horse?"

"No, I own her, but she was special to someone that I know. I want her to be here if she ever comes back."

"Your lady?"

"I wish," Jonah said softly as he walked away.

One day as they were standing in the smithy getting ready to close for the day, Molly walked in with little Mack wrapped in her arms.

"Jonah, can you come by and fix the lock on my front door. It's broken and I don't want to leave my door unlocked. I'm scared enough staying alone as it is," she chuckled nervously.

"I will fix it right now. Go on home and I will bring a new lock by in just a few minutes."

"Thanks, I appreciate it."

Jonah noticed the look on Ian's face. He looked spellbound. He thought he probably should straighten the boy out, and let him know that she was taken.

"This is Ian Campbell. He is going to run my place while I am gone. And this is Molly Reeves and little Mack." Jonah said, turning to Ian. "Her husband has already left to join the forces."

"Am so pleased to meet you, Ma'am. Looks like you might have a wee one all wrapped up in those quilts," he said, as he looked at the bundle she held.

"Yes, my son, Mack," she replied, as she pulled back the covers for him to see.

"He's a fine boy, Mrs. Reeves," he commented as he tickled the baby's chin.

"Thank you, Mr. Campbell, nice to meet you," she answered, smiling "I will talk to you later, Jonah." As she walked away Ian watched her. Jonah tapped him on the shoulder. "She's married, so you can pick your chin up off of your chest."

"I knew that! She had a little one. But I do appreciate beautiful women."

"I can see!" Jonah chuckled. "You might help Clay look out for Molly while we are gone. Mack would appreciate his wife being looked after with great respect!"

"I will respect her Jonah. I think she is a fine looking woman, but I would never tramp on someone else's territory." Jonah believed he meant it, but he might put a bug in Clay's ear to watch the watcher.

*   *

In March, 1862, Jonah left his home of the last fourteen years of his life with Simon beside him. It was going to be quite awhile before he saw it again.

The war had been going on for over eleven months. It had taken a lot of talking to keep Simon from going right away. He had hoped that he was wrong and it would end soon, but Jonah had lost all hope that it would be short-lived. He dreaded every step that his horse took away from there. He had done many things in his lifetime that he didn't want to do, but he thought this was the worst. Besides leaving his home and St. Jo, he was leaving the few people he called friends. There was always the chance that he or Simon might not return.

115

Jonah soon saw that not everybody there knew how to ride or shoot well. He knew if they won this war it would be pure luck if the rest of the army was like this.

Riding with Major White's Prairie Scouts, Jonah and Simon along with five thousand men from other troops joined Fremont's troops, making about twenty thousand men. They rode into Springfield and released Union soldiers that had been captured, then made it a Union stronghold. Sleeping on the ground in the summer months wasn't so bad, but when winter arrived it would be different.

*   *

Winter came in hard and cold, and some days moving around was the only thing that kept them warm. Ice sometimes gathered on their beards and eyelashes. Some of the recruits barely had enough clothes to wear and weren't able to keep warm. Many had shoddy shoes on their feet. The only good thing about winter was there were fewer battles. Most troops settled in for the winter. They kept to their tents and kept the fire going.

At night when Jonah lay in his bed, the only thing that kept him warm were thoughts of Sunny. He had never truly longed for anyone since he had been a small boy. He used to lay in his stinky bed at night, and ached for the love of a parent. He could feel Sunny's gentle touch, and see the smile she bestowed upon him with that sparkle in her eyes.

He had been in hellholes before, but since being an adult he had control over his life. He promised himself that he would never live in a filthy place, sleep on a rotting bed, or let anyone mean anything to him. Clay, Joseph and Mack had become friends, but they hadn't overtaken his life. Simon took more from him, but he handled it with ease.

His love for Sunny turned him inside out. He needed her like he hadn't ever needed anyone in his adult life. It was more than wanting a woman. She dug at his heart with sharp thorns. She loved him, and he had no doubts about that, but would she have been strong enough to put up with all the problems he would have brought her. How deep was her love, how strong? Did he sell her short? Her father seemed to think she was strong and faithful enough. Maybe he would have been hung by some mob, but at least he would have had her for awhile.

The men would cuddle up in whatever they could find and eat their small rations. Jonah could hear boys cry at night. Their bold honor to fight was lost in the miserable existence. It didn't take much to make the young men want to be back home, in the warmth and love of their families. Simon was even questioning himself, wondering if there could have been a better way to help his people. Jonah had to talk him through the rough times. They had been in this war almost a year, and it seemed an eternity.

President Lincoln lost his young son, Willie, not in this war, but from polluted drinking water. As horrible as things were, Jonah knew he wasn't the only miserable person.

♥

Chapter 15

The spring of 1863 found Sunny looking outside at trees turning green. She saw Levi coming up the walk, carrying the mail as usual. She always looked forward to her letters. She hadn't received many letters from Jonah lately.

"Is there a letter from Jonah," she asked, as she opened the door for her brother. Patches started barking at his feet, wanting some attention from him.

"Not from Jonah, but one from Mom. You know it was about time for one. She's always faithful," he said, handing her the letter. Sunny ripped it open and read it.

Dear Daughter,

The war is taking up everyone's life in one way or another. Molly is so scared to stay by herself that she sometimes comes over with the baby and spends the night in your old room. We told her she could move in here, but she wants to stay in the house Mack built her. Everybody made the best of Christmas as they could, but with husbands, sons and brothers gone to war, it was not the best of times.

Doc was home for a short while from the hospital ship. That steamboat picks up wounded and cares for them until they can be taken to a base hospital, then it turns around and makes another journey back.

It is finally warming up now that spring is here. The winter seemed so long. I am sorry I haven't written in a while, but we have been so busy. The women from the church are making bandages, quilts and gowns for the hospitals. They are in need all of the time. Anything we can do makes us feel like we help in some small way.

I miss you, Sunny, and wish you were home. I know your brother will take care of you the best he can, but I hear that Virginia is getting its share of war too. The church has prayer vigils for the soldiers every day. We send them up for Jonah and Simon daily, as I am sure you do. Take care.

With all my love, Your Mother.

Sunny's heart beat raced whenever she thought about Jonah fighting. Tears slipped from her eyes.

She held her mother's letter in her hand, bent her head and asked God to watch over them. She could stand it no longer, she had to go home. It was time.

"Sun, what's the matter?" Levi asked, his voice filled with questions.

"I'm going home." she said, with tears still in her eyes.

"Are you crazy? We are in the middle of a war."

"I have to go, Levi. Jonah might need me and I want to be close to him."

Levi took her hand and sat down beside her. "I do understand, but this is not the time for you to be traveling alone. If nothing else, there could be lots of soldiers traveling, and we can't imagine who else. War brings out opportunists of all kinds, everything from scalawags to murderers. It's just not safe right now. Wait until summer and maybe I will get a chance to escort you home."

"No, I have to go now. Molly is scared to stay alone so I can stay with her and wait for Jonah."

Shaking his head in exasperation, Levi said, "Okay, but I'm not letting you go alone. Grandfather has lots of tough men on the docks. I will see who he can trust to take you home."

As it turned out, her grandfather decided to take her home himself, with a couple of tough men as guards. All the way home on the train, the wheels seemed to sing to her saying; I'm coming home, back to you Jonah. She knew it was really her heart that was singing the song, but she was filled with joy. She prayed for his safety constantly.

She spent more time talking to her grandfather than she ever had. She began to tell him about Jonah. He told her there was a time he would have agreed with all those narrow-minded people. When Bess married Isaiah he thought it was the worst thing she could have done. He would never amount to anything, as far as he was concerned. But he found out how wrong he was. Grandfather told her, he realized that her parents knew how to love, not only each other, but their children and other people as well. "I wish all of my children had the spirit and values that my Bess did. I don't know how she turned out so fine, but it wasn't anything I did, I'm sure."

The locomotive whistle drew her from her thoughts. She was almost home, except home was with Jonah. He had to come home for a short break sometime and she was going to be there. She had written her mother and told her when she planned to arrive, but the train was already late. They had to wait a few hours to repair some track before they could leave some little station in the middle of nowhere.

She knew her father would be listening for the loud whistle coming into town. When the train came to a screeching stop, Sunny was ready to get off. As she disembarked, there stood her parents, Clay, and Molly with baby Mack. Tears sprang to her eyes. She knew this was where she belonged. She ran to them with Patches following close behind. She hugged them all one at a time with tears flowing down her cheeks.

Her grandfather stayed a week and visited. If it hadn't been for the war going on it would have been wonderful. He left her the greatest gift in the world. Wait until she told Jonah.

She moved in with Molly, and everyone kept an eye on them. She crooned over little Mack, thinking she could almost have had one of her own by now, if Jonah would have married her back when. Molly was less scared with Sunny around.

Sunny had her old spirit and drive back. Her one objective was to do what she could until Jonah got home. Who knew how long this war would last, but she kept her faith in God, believing He would bring Jonah back to her.

Sunny spent her time rolling bandages to send to military hospitals, for they had to use corn husks for bandages from time to time. She, Molly and several other women in town met at Molly's house and made quilts besides knitting scarves and socks. They baked cookies and made candies to send to men. It all kept her from going crazy thinking about Jonah. She also worried about Simon, Mack and other men and boys from their community. They kept their name on a board. Doc came back from the hospital ship that transported the wounded to and from the military hospital in St. Louis. Jefferson Barracks had been converted into a 3000 bed hospital and was fast becoming a burial ground as well. He would bring back any names that were on the wounded list. So far they hadn't had many, but everybody held their breath.

*   *

It was early fall and the war had been going on for over two years, and Jonah had been gone almost that long. Sunny thought the war would be over by now and Jonah would be home, but it was still raging. Doc escorted several soldiers home to recoup from their wounds, or even worse, to bury them. Those were the lucky ones, because many were buried on the battlefield far from home. Some families might never know what happened to their loved ones until after the war, and they never would return.

Sometimes Sunny would stop by and visit Gypsy at the stables, making her feel closer to Jonah. That's where she met Ian Campbell. She assumed he had been in America quite a while. He told her when he was young they called him Rusty, because his hair was the color of rust when he was born, but turned more brown as he got older. Clay informed him who she was. Jonah left special orders

121

that Gypsy was never to be rented or sold, that she belonged to Sunny.

Everybody teased Molly because Ian was infatuated by her. They told her if Mack didn't come home soon, Ian would kidnap her. Everybody could hear Ian singing tunes as he worked, and sometimes he would sing of his beautiful Irish maiden. They all thought maybe it was Molly that he was singing about. It seemed so different there without Jonah and Simon.

While she was out, she would drop by and see Sheriff Clay's wife, Marie. Their little boy, Jason, was little Mack's age. Patches always took up with babies, since he had spent so much time with Samuel. Sunny would play with Jacob, and Patches would have his nose stuck right in the middle of it all.

"I'm so glad you came back, Sunny. We all missed you. I know an idiot who has been one big heartache," Marie said, shaking her head with exasperation.

"I hope everyone is right because if he comes back here I'm not going to let him get away again."

"Good for you."

"I'd better get back. Molly doesn't like to be alone. She's so worried about Mack. She doesn't hear from him very often. Sometimes the mail isn't great and we don't get letters like we should," she sighed. I don't even know where to write to Jonah anymore and he doesn't know I'm home."

"Don't worry; we are all praying for our young men."

As Sunny left Marie's house, it was getting close to dusk. She hadn't meant to stay so long. Sunny was usually very careful about being on the streets alone and was hurrying home when she spotted a rider coming into town. Grabbing Patches, she ducked behind a bush in someone's yard. She was horrified when she saw a scalp dangling from his horse's reins. Sunny heard the stories about the raiders who did that. She shook like a leaf, but he passed by her and proceeded on down the street.

122

When he was out of sight she hugged Patches close to her and ran as fast as she could go. When she pounded on the door for Molly to open it, she was breathing hard. Sunny knew most of it was from fear, not exertion and almost fell inside when the door was opened.

"What in the world is wrong?" Molly exclaimed.

"I saw a raider come into town."

"How do you know it was a raider?" Molly asked, with eyes filled with fright.

"He had a human scalp hanging from the bridle and he was wearing a blue jacket, just like all the stories we have heard about them."

"What are we going to do?"

"There was only one, but to be safe, we will blow out all the lanterns, close the curtains, and only light a small candle. I will get the gun Papa gave me and keep it close by. If we hear any noise, grab the baby and hide in a closet. I will protect you even if I have to kill him." They knew she was talking more bravely than she felt. Sunny wondered if she could actually kill someone if she had to. She hoped if it came down to it, she would do what had to be done.

They peeked from behind the curtain several times, but nothing happened. They decided they had become overly anxious, but neither of the women slept well that night, and were very glad when morning came. Sunny related her story to Clay the next day, thinking he would laugh at her.

"You're right. He was here and dropped by the saloon. The man was by himself, so he must be coming from somewhere or going to a certain place, or he wouldn't have been alone. We are not sure if he was a border ruffian. I talked to him and asked some questions, but he didn't give me any real answers. He rode out shortly afterwards. I think he knew he had wandered into the wrong place.

"I hope Jonah doesn't ever have to cross those guys," she said.

"I hope not either."

"I wish he would come home."

"I know, so do I." Clay said, as he reached over and patted her arm.

She prayed daily for all their safety.

In April Doc escorted a fallen soldier home. He was barely nineteen. He gave news to two other families that they had wounded sons. When they were able to travel, he would bring them home. Sunny was sad because she knew the family of a young man who had been killed in battle. It was so hard to comfort his family knowing what grief they were going through. She thanked God that it wasn't Jonah, and felt ashamed that she sensed relief over someone else's sorrow.

Less than a month later Doc brought Mack home to Molly in a coffin. Sunny went with her to see him at the undertaker's. When Molly saw her husband lying there so cold and still, she fell to the floor weeping. Sunny held and rocked the young widow in her arms and couldn't keep the tears from flowing from her own eyes. She knew she needed to be strong for the family. This was just the beginning of heartache for her best friend. Sunny wished she had an answer for Molly, but she knew she would never forget Mack. This horrible war was already leaving so many scars and it had barely started. She wanted Jonah home.

They buried Mack in the church cemetery on a beautiful summer day. The clouds were white and fluffy. Just by looking at the world nobody would have known what a sad day it was. Sunny knew Molly was in shock, for she didn't shed any more tears. She smiled and nodded in a dazed-like state. It was as if she was there in body, but her heart, mind and soul were far removed.

Sunny held little Mack. She hugged him close feeling sad that he would never know his father. She didn't know how they made it through the funeral, talking to all the people who were there to celebrate Mack's life.

Sunny noticed Ian. He watched Molly with misery in his eyes. She knew in that moment that Ian loved Molly and that he felt her misery, and was helpless to make things all right for her. Ian had become a good friend to Molly and her since Sunny had come home. He checked on them many times to make sure they were alright. He would stay for supper sometimes, joking and telling stories, making them laugh. He played with little Mack. Everybody talked about Ian being infatuated with Molly, but Sunny saw that he deeply loved her.

Molly's parents came to help her. They wanted the baby and her to come home with them, but she said she was staying in the beautiful house that Mack had built for her.

Sunny knew Molly would fall apart as soon as the shock wore off. She was right, for Molly hardly talked and she rarely ate. Shortly the tears started and wouldn't stop. Sunny didn't leave her side. Molly was in deep sorrow. When she wasn't sobbing, she slept from exhaustion. Sunny took care of little Mack and his mother. She asked her mother and father to help her, so Bess helped Sunny run the house and take care of the baby.

Isaiah got Molly to talk to him about everything she knew and remembered about Mack. Isaiah listened while she shared her memories. It helped her to handle her grief better. She began to hold her baby again and slowly started to accept her great loss. It was going to take a long time, but she was starting to take hold of her situation. Sunny knew Molly was far from well. She heard her crying at night. Please, Lord, let this come to an end fast. Sunny prayed for Jonah constantly. Ian checked with Sunny often to ask about Molly, but did not ask to see her.

Sunny went to the general store to pick up a few things, and stopped by to greet Gypsy for a minute. She wasn't in the pen. Sunny walked to the smithy and found Ian sitting on one of Jonah's nail kegs looking like a lost little boy. She watched him for a minute, but he never did notice her there. She sat her supplies down inside the door and walked over in front of him.

125

"Sunny, lass! I didn't even hear you come in. How can I help you?" he said, getting up.

"What is going on here? The Ian I know can't sit still for a minute, always laughing and telling jokes. What's the matter?"

He shook his head from side to side.

"Tell me what's going on. Is it about you being in love with Molly?

"What makes you think that?" he said, looking at her in surprise.

"I know! I love someone, so it's easy to see it in other people."

"I never meant to fall in love with her. When I knew I felt things for her that was not my right, the wicked man inside of me, made thoughts run through me from time to time. Her husband dying would be the only way. Isn't that terrible of me?" he said, looking away from her.

"We are only human Ian, and you don't know Mack. If you did, you would never have thought that. You certainly didn't have the power to make it so. That was God's decision. Molly has a long road of grief ahead of her, and she can use your friendship, and mine. Don't feel guilty for a passing thought. God brought Mack into her life for a season, and we don't know the why of such things. In time, if you and Molly are meant to be together, you will be. I have that same hope and faith where Jonah is concerned. We just have to hang on and keep on."

"Thanks Sunny. I couldn't bear to see her. I was afraid she could see the terrible thought that I had. "

"Believe me; you look as miserable as she does. You have more empathy for her than you realize. Just be her friend for now. Things will happen when they should."

"I will. What did you come in for?"

"Where is Gypsy?"

"I heard that some people have been stealing horses. We think they are doing it to sell or give to soldiers. I decided to hide Gypsy out of plain sight. Since I'm staying at Jonah's cabin, I put her in the pasture up there where nobody can easily see her from the road."

"That's a good idea. Thanks for being so thoughtful," she said, as she reached up and tapped him on the cheek. "Remember, no more guilt. It's a waste of time."

He winked at her and shook his head. "I'll do my best."

Ian started stopping by and spending more time with Molly and Sunny. He turned out to be one of the best things to help Molly along. He talked to her about Mack, like he was still alive, and let Molly tell him stories of their courtship and marriage. He took her to the cemetery when she wanted to go and put flowers on his grave. He held her when she cried. He laughed with her and became the same jovial Ian. Little Mack was walking and Ian played with him and chased him. Ian wrestled around with him until he was exhausted and happy. Molly still had bad times, but she was beginning to patch her life back together. Like everybody else, she hated the war with good reason.

♥

Chapter 16
1863

Jonah was weary. He felt like he had fought in this cursed war for years. Simon had been missing for four months. After a battle he was nowhere to be found. Jonah looked frantically among the dead. He later found out that some of their unit had been cut off during the skirmish. The very reason that he went to war was for Simon, now he was missing. Jonah refused to believe he was dead.

He would be home in a few hours, and he was ready for a furlough. He needed some peace at home since he had dug more graves than he ever wanted to, saw more young half-grown boys die, and had to even kill some.

Simon became a man in the last year. He filled out, grew several inches, and did some of the hardest things a man had to do. That kept hope in Jonah's heart that Simon would take care of himself. He would find him somewhere, someday.

He rode into St. Jo about dusk. It was quiet, and that suited him fine. He put Warrior in the stable, and talked to Ian a few minutes. Ian gracefully told Jonah he would stay in the barn loft while he was home. Jonah stopped by the general store and picked up some food. After a bite to eat, Jonah walked out onto his porch and watched the setting sun. It was beautiful. He had seen it from many different places, but it never looked so good as it did here.

It had been almost two years since he last saw Sunny. He wondered if the ache in his heart would ever go away. Her old letters kept him going. He read them so many times that they were thin and torn.

She had been like sunshine warming him from all the cold years he had lived. She awakened something real and worthy that he hadn't known existed. He couldn't forget anything about her, from her sparkling blue eyes to her flashing smile. If she only knew how much he needed her. If he lived to be a very old man he would never forget that she loved him. It was the greatest gift that her God had ever bestowed upon him. Sometimes when he was settling down for the night, he would write Sunny. He decided not to mail them because they were so full of despair and hopelessness. He didn't want to send her those kinds of letters.

Clay hurried down the street to get Sunny. Joseph had told him Jonah stopped in and got some food. He could wait until tomorrow to see him, but she needed to see him tonight. He pounded on the door, and yelled for her to open up. She stood looking at him with fear in her eyes.

"What's the matter," she asked, anxiously.

"Jonah just got home. Get your tail over to his house. I will walk you to the edge of the lane."

Sunny put her hand over her smiling mouth, and her eyes were big with anticipation. "I will get my garb on," she said, as Clay stepped inside to wait for her. They planned this months ago. She got some boy's clothes and an old floppy hat. If anyone saw her go to Jonah's house, they would just think it was some lad.

As Clay and Sunny headed for Jonah's house, her heart was pounding in her chest. He had to still love her like everyone said. He had to, or her heart would break all over again. Clay stopped at the bottom of the lane. "You can go from here. Tell that stubborn friend of mine to come and see me tomorrow. Good luck," he said as he winked at her.

Sunny walked up the short lane to the house. As she got closer she saw Jonah standing on the front porch. It was almost dark, but the light from the house surrounded him, and she could see him plainly. He looked so good to her. He was standing against the porch railing, just looking out over the valley below. She had an answer for them that her grandfather had given her. Would Jonah go along with it? She continued to walk up to the house.

Jonah hadn't slept in a decent bed for months, so he wondered why he wasn't falling into his bed. He knew he never really appreciated his home before. It had taken him years to get one, and he missed it. There was only one thing he wanted more, and she wasn't here.

While looking out through the trees he drank a cup of coffee. The moon was glowing, and stars were bright. He never appreciated the sight more than tonight. He caught a movement through the trees coming up the path to the house. He didn't have his gun with him, but he decided to wait and see who or what it was before he got excited. He saw a person coming up to the porch. It looked like a young, skinny boy. He squinted into the dark as the lad stepped onto the porch into the light, and removed his hat. He was spellbound. He couldn't take his eyes off of her. It was Sunny!

"Jonah," she said, with tears streaming down her face.

He didn't know if he grabbed her, or she stepped into his arms, but he was holding her. His sweet Sunny! She threw her arms around him, and sobbed into his chest. A big lump was in his throat and he held her as tight as possible kissing her face, and neck. Oh yes, he remembered the feel of her, her scent, and her softness. He recalled it everyday that she had been away from him.

"Oh, Sweetheart, I can't believe it's you. I have dreamed of you everyday." She looked up at him, and he bent and kissed her lips, picking her up in his arms he walked to the rocking chair on the porch. He held her in his arms, rubbing his roughened cheek against her smooth one.

"I love you," she said, simply.

"I love you too," he said, tenderly, looking into her wet eyes. "What are you doing in St. Jo?" What are you doing dressed like a boy?"

"I came back months ago. I had to be here when you came home. Are you going to send me away again?"

"No, I can't. I don't want to live without you."

"I don't want to live without you either." Jonah had to kiss her again and again. He just couldn't get enough of her. She was what he was born for. She was what had melted his hard heart. She was all he needed to make life matter. There was no way that he could let her go.

"Are you going to marry me?"

"Someday I hope," he said, smiling at her bluntness.

"Not good enough!"

"What do you mean," he said, looking at her in puzzlement.

"We are getting married tomorrow if I have to get Clay down here with a shotgun."

"Tomorrow," he said, smiling broadly.

"Tomorrow. I'm moving in here tomorrow. It's up to you if you want me to be an honest woman or not," she said, with her tear stained eyes.

"Where are we doing this?"

"At Molly's house. We can get a few friends to come. Papa can marry us."

"We can't Sweetheart because nothing has changed."

"Oh yes it has. I told you I would find an answer and I have."

"Okay, what is the answer?"

"First, I have to ask you a question. Do you love me enough to live somewhere else?"

"Anywhere as long as you're with me"

"My grandfather owns five hundred acres of land in Denver City that he gave us for a wedding present. He says new towns are springing up all over the country and are being settled by all kinds of people. Out west nobody cares what your nationality is. Everybody is working hard to make it, and are just happy to have a neighbor within a few miles. So see, that's our answer. Move to Denver City and build our life there."

"It will be a hard life, are you sure you want to do that?"

"I don't care as long as we can be together without people telling us we can't love each other. Are you willing?"

"You bet I am. As soon as this war is over we will head for Kansas Territory." He answered as he pulled her back into his arms. He could finally have her. Maybe that would work.

"We are still getting married tomorrow."

"How is that going to work? I only have two weeks until I have to go back."

"I'm not asking you to give up the war. I know you have to go back. I am asking you to spend every minute that we can together until you have to leave. I don't want to wait, Jonah, I want to marry you now. It will be a secret among just a few of our closest friends. I can stay here and not leave until you have to go back. Then I can sneak back to Molly's in my boy's clothes. Nobody has to know where I am."

"And what if you are expecting a baby when I leave, what then?"

"Then I will go to Denver City and wait for you there."

"By yourself, there's no way."

"My parents will go with me. My grandfather hired someone to build a cabin already. My grandfather probably has a pretty elaborate idea for a simple cabin."

Jonah didn't know if all of Sunny's ideas would turn out right, but he had to do it. He couldn't let her go again. If there was any chance for them, he had to take it.

They sat where they were and talked about how they had pined over each other. She told him she had been living with Molly and that Mack had died. Jonah was rocked by the news. Mack was good friend and so full of life. Jonah fought for the wrong reasons but Mack had fought for the right ones. He told her about the hell they had seen; young boys getting killed. They held each other and talked about everything in their hearts. When it got late Jonah walked her home.

The next morning Jonah decided to go see Isaiah.

"Come in stranger," Isaiah said, as he led him into the parlor.

"I wondered if I could talk to you for a minute" Jonah asked, as he nervously moved his hat around in his hands. He had never been in a position where the answers this man gave him would mean so much. He knew if he objected, he could never marry Sunny outside of his blessings. There was too much against them to start with and he could never put a rift between Sunny and her beloved family.

Jonah moved to a chair and sat down across from Isaiah. "I love your daughter," he stated, as he looked at him. He watched him smile, and that made Jonah relax a little.

"Do you think that's a surprise to me?"

"No, but Sunny and I want to get married"

"That's no surprise either," he said with a chuckle.

"Well the surprise might be that she wants to get married today."

"I kinda got a hint of that from my daughter. She said if she could talk you into it. So did she?"

"I love her, Isaiah."

"I know you do,"

"I promise that I will always do my best by her."

"I know that too, son."

"You could accept me as her husband knowing what all is against us?"

"Jonah, you are a good man. I agree that you will have some tough times. Sunny has never backed down from what she believes in, and she believes in you. She loves you and the biggest reason I don't object is that I know how much you love her back."

"It's easier for me to love her. I will never understand why she loves me."

"You sell yourself short because of the blood that runs through your veins. I hope you will see in your lifetime that what a man is, will be a lot more important than where he comes from. If I had to pick my daughter's husband I would want her to have the kind of love that her mother and I shared. That's the most important thing I wish for her, and I think you're the one who can fulfill that dream. Welcome to the family, Jonah. We will be honored to call you our son-in-law."

Jonah had to swallow around the lump in his throat. If it took everything in him, he would not disappoint this man. Loving her was no problem. He would do anything to keep her safe and make her happy.

"I know that I should wait until after the war is over, but I don't want to. I am being selfish, I know. I could leave her a widow, and that would be hard for her."

"You would leave her with wonderful memories, and that would mean more to her than waiting, I think. Don't you?"

"I hope you're right." Jonah said, smiling.

"I think I am," he said as he got up and yelled for Bess. When she came into the room he told her they were having a wedding today.

♥

Chapter 17

Jonah Alexander and Sarah Markley became man and wife in Molly's parlor. He had never seen such a beautiful bride, probably because she was his. She wore an ordinary white dress with little blue flowers on it and a white frilly hat. He watched her come down the stairs and his heart was full of love for her. She was a mixture of love, courage, humor, and compassion. She may have been nine years younger than he, but she had been his teacher in many ways. God, please don't ever let her regret loving me, he prayed silently. Only Clay, Marie, Ian, and Molly were there except for her parents.

Isaiah led them through their wedding vows and pronounced them bound together for as long as they both lived. Everybody wished them a long marriage and happy life together. They both kept the worry of war buried deep on this special day. Jonah was going to be home for two weeks, and Sunny would love him with all of her being for that length of time.

After a nice meal and wedding cake for dessert, the new married couple went home. They talked while watching the beautiful sunset from their front porch. Jonah held his young wife in his arms, hardly believing it had really happened. He had dreamed this dream for so long and needed to pinch himself to see if it was real. He leaned down and kissed her tenderly.

"Should I get ready for bed?" she asked, looking at him shyly.

"Only if you're ready," he replied, as he placed his hand against her face affectionately. "I can wait if you're not."

"I've been waiting for this night for a long time," she said, as she reached up and kissed him adoringly, and went inside. Jonah leaned against the post, looking at the stars. He was nervous. He wanted to make love to his wife, but he didn't want to bring back some awful memories for her. He hoped he could be tender and loving enough. She was still innocent where intimacy was concerned. What she had experienced had been violence, nothing to do with marriage. Sweat popped out on his forehead from being scared. Jonah walked into the parlor and sat down in the rocking chair. He looked up as she opened the bedroom door and walked out. Sunny stood there, wearing a soft blue nightgown with her hair down. She was adorable, and he wanted her.

"I wondered why my husband wasn't anxious to come into the bedroom," she asked, concerned.

"Oh, he is anxious! Just scared."

"Of what?" she asked, surprised.

"I am afraid I will remind you of that day in the hills, with the kid," he said, softly.

"Oh, Jonah," she said, as she walked over and sat on his lap. She kissed him and looked into his eyes "There is a lot of difference between this and that. I'm not a child; I know what goes on between married people. I'm excited, but I would be lying if I said I wasn't nervous. I've dreamed about this part of our relationship. It's part of our love." Jonah rose from the chair holding her in his arms. "Let's make our dreams come true," he said as he carried her into the bedroom.

The newly married couple never ran out of things to talk about. She was interesting and funny. Simon was the only hitch. Jonah still worried about him. Sunny assured him that he had raised Simon well, teaching him many skills that would help the young man. She prayed for Simon daily and Jonah began to join in with her. He told God he wouldn't ask him for anything concerning Simon, but just give him the answers he needed to know if he was still alive. The nights were more beautiful than he could have imagined. With the wonder of it all came a fear like he had never known. He thought he loved her as much as possible, but after just a few days of marriage, he loved her even more. It would kill him if he ever lost her.

He started having dreams and couldn't sleep. Jonah would quietly get out of bed and go out onto the porch. He knew his dreams were coming from his fears. In them

Sunny would walk away from him while he begged her to come back. She would walk into the dark, leaving him forlorn and dejected. His heart would be racing when he woke, then he would feel her warm body against him. He knew it was a dream, but it was happening often. Jonah stood looking into the night, wondering what his future held. He sure hadn't had much in the past, but he had something wonderful now, and feared losing it.

"Why is my new husband coming out here at night, I wonder?" Sunny asked, quietly.

Jonah turned around and sat on the railing, taking her hand. She moved closer looking at him anxiously.

"Are you unhappy?" she asked fearful of his answer.

"No, not at all," he answered, as he pulled her closer.

"Then tell me what's wrong."

He looked down at their joined hands and started caressing hers with his thumb.

"I'm scared."

"Of what? The war?" she asked, concerned.

"Something a man is not supposed to admit. I'm scared of losing you. I've never worried about losing anything in my whole life, until you. I'm dreaming that you leave me and I become this worthless excuse for a human being without you."

She slipped into his arms and looked at him. "Why do you have this terrible image of yourself? You're a wonderful man and I love you so much. Clay chose you for his best friend. My dad respects you. Mack and Ian considered you a good friend. We both know how Simon feels about you. It's all about your childhood, my darling, but God brought you through it."

"I never thought God helped me when I was a kid. I have really been trying to read His word and understand what He is all about, but I still have doubts, I guess."

"You didn't see Him help you? What about an old cowboy that taught you how to ride and rope, and care for horses. How about an experienced gunslinger who taught you how to use a gun? How about a German man who taught you how to be a blacksmith? Do you think God didn't bring those people into your life? It was up to you how you reacted, and you used all your lessons well. God brought my dad here, and I came along, so what do you think about that?"

"Maybe He was around. Maybe I had better thank Him after all."

"Maybe you had better. As far as me leaving you, that will be the day! I love you so much Jonah. Have faith in me. I am a grown woman, and I know what I feel. When we have about a dozen kids and I'm old and gray, you'll remember this silly conversation."

"I do have faith in you. I will be thankful for every day that I get to spend with you. You remember that, when I am old and gray," he said, smiling.

"I'm scared to leave you alone. Promise me you will be careful when I am gone," Jonah said, passionately as he pulled his wife into his arms.

"I will. I promise to take extra care. I have my dad, Clay, and Ian, who all look out for me. You will be in much more danger than I will. Please watch out for yourself. We can't lose each other now, Jonah," she whispered as she clung to him tighter.

The night before he left neither one slept much during the night. They made plans for moving to Denver City after the war. He made arrangements to sell his home and business to Ian. If Sunny found that she was going to have a baby, she and her parents would go on to Denver City without him, and he would follow when the war was over. They couldn't seem to tell each other enough how they felt. It would be a long time before they would be able to say it again. What if something happened to one of them? How would they go on? They had gone through so much to get this far.

Jonah rode away the next morning, looking back every few seconds until he could no longer see Sunny waving bye to him. She sobbed and clung to him when he left, and he wanted to do the same. He prayed that this hellish war would end soon.

*   *

They came upon the train shortly after Bloody Bill Anderson and his cutthroat gang had murdered almost everyone on it, and left the dead strung everywhere. There were people lying in the street and on the porch of the station. The gang waited until the train came to a stop at the station before they attacked. Jonah would never get used to slaughtered men that they had to bury.

They fought in the battle at Boonville, giving the Union Army the victory.

Colonel J.T. Hughes' confederate forces took Independence at dawn, giving them the rule in the Kansas City area. Again in August, one of the bloodiest battles in Missouri took place. The Union attacked Lone Jack with 800 men. The next morning a counter attack from the Confederacy left 200 men dying or dead, with the Confederacy taking the victory and leaving homes and businesses burned to the ground.

In October Quantrill burned Shawnee, Kansas to the ground. It also brought in the completion of the telegraph. Communications were rapid now. It also brought the decline of the Pony Express. Only one mailbag had been lost and one rider killed in the eighteen months of the Pony Express, but even with such good results, it now died. They couldn't begin to compete with the telegraph. The company went bankrupt. The owners lost the mail contract and ended up penniless.

The war dragged along and it didn't look like it would wind down. Young men were dying as families were burned out of their homes. Food and medicine were scarce, and yet the war continued.

The last year had taken its toll on Jonah's soul. It seemed to be one dreary battle after another. He hadn't seen Sunny in months. Every time he got close enough to make a fast trip home, the war would lead him in a different direction. He wanted a day with her, just one lousy day. When a letter caught up with him, it was weeks old. He didn't know how many were floating around and how many of his got to her. They spent weeks in Arkansas and even Oklahoma. Things were no better there, but he was glad to be back in Missouri. Just being here made him feel better.

He knew they were getting primed for another battle. They watched the Confederate army moving their way behind them for days. They expected gunfire at any time. Jonah felt the tension in the air and in his bones. He hoped they weren't heavily outnumbered. Then gunfire broke into the silence and he knew what was coming. It was time for another battle.

Jonah sat on the hillside trying to stop the bleeding in his chest. He had been nicked and scraped before, but he got a bad wound this time. Jonah took a scarf from around his neck and pressed it to the wound. The soldier looked at the smoke surrounding him. He didn't even know who won, and right now it didn't even matter. He was getting weak. It was strange, but he felt a peace. Even stranger he knew it was God. On a battlefield with dying people all around him, God gave him a peace that he really did understand. He looked up, and tears started to run down his face. "Lord. I know who you are now. Forgive me. If I die here today, I want to thank you for the people you put in my life, especially Sunny. She may have been my wife for such a short time, and Lord, I do want to grow old with her, but if this is the end, I will be thankful for her." He was getting lightheaded, and he slowly lay down on the grass. His eyes closed, and he felt like he was drifting on a cloud. *"Get up Jonah," a voice said to him. "Get up. People need you. Go help your comrades."*

"I'm too tired," he said, yet he wasn't sure if he said it or thought it.

"Get up, Jonah, someone needs your help. Now!"

Jonah drug his body up to a sitting position, and looked out to the wounded boys, moaning and crying. He stumbled to his feet and started across the field. The first person he came upon was a young boy in gray. He squatted down and the boy grabbed his hand.

"Forgive me Jonah, for hating you," he said between gasps of pain.

Jonah looked into the face of the young deputy, Hayden. He was shocked. People like him made his life miserable at times, and now he was asking for forgiveness.

"Forgive him, Jonah." The voice said. "I forgave you!" At that moment, Jonah knew that with the power of God he could forgive. Hayden was just a boy, and he had only hated because he had been taught to. In the end Hayden didn't get what he wanted after all. But Jonah had been blessed. He had some great friends and a beautiful wife. He could forgive.

"No problem, Hayden. Forget it."

"Then you forgive me?" he asked, with breath, gasping for more air.

"Sure thing. Let me get you patched up and see if we can't get you some help."

"I think I'm going to die." Jonah looked at his wound, and knew his bleeding had to be stopped too. He took his kerchief off, but that wasn't going to do it. He jerked his pocket knife out and cut Hayden's pant legs off and bound them over his wound.

"Lie still now and I will get some help." It took Jonah a while, but he found some men to take him to the medical wagon. As they carried him away, he heard Hayden thank him. Jonah stood there, feeling really good, just before he passed out on the battlefield.

♥

Chapter 18
1863

The weather turned and Sunny looked forward to the cold. If all the troops settled in for the winter, maybe Jonah would get a furlough. She hadn't seen him since the few days they had together, right after their marriage. She slipped her cape on and told Molly she was going to see Clay. Since the telegraph, he got news fast about the war. Doc sent a wire to Clay if he came across anyone from St. Jo that was hurt or killed.

"Hello, Clay. Any kind of news?"

"Nothing today. No news nowadays is good news."

"I know. I hope Jonah gets a furlough soon. I haven't received a letter since early September."

"I wouldn't worry about that. The mail doesn't get through much now."

Sunny paced back and forth in front of the window. She finally sat on a chair, looking desperate.

"You look worn out, Sunny. Maybe you need to settle down and get some rest."

"I'm alright. I get this way sometimes, especially after I have bad dreams."

"Did you have a bad dream?"

"I have them a lot. I know it's fear for Jonah, but I'm always agitated for a couple of days after having one."

"Settle down and take a deep breath. Jonah is a tough guy."

"I know, but that doesn't mean he can't be hurt, Clay."

Clay walked over and helped her to her feet. "Go home, and get some rest. You are always busy doing something. You need to be in good health when Jonah comes home. Take care of yourself. Now scoot, and think about good things."

Sunny smiled at Clay and nodded her head and left.

Clay didn't tell her he worried about Jonah too. It wouldn't have helped any.

A middle-aged man with a slight limp named Bradley Urich ran the telegraph office. He was good at his job; but waited until he could get a runner to deliver a telegram if it wasn't urgent. He wouldn't leave his desk. Clay walked over toward the end of the day to pick up any messages. If there was an emergency Bradley would yell at someone on the street and get them to deliver it.

He decided to grab his coat and check the day's telegrams. Clay knew it was hardly ever good news when they got one, and he hated having to ride out and inform a family of a death. Clay knew St. Jo was in better condition than most towns.

"Any news from the fighting front today, Bradley?" Clay asked, as he stepped into the office out of the biting cold weather.

"Fraid so, Clay. You won't like this one," Bradley said, as he handed it to Clay.

Fear gripped Clay as he grabbed the telegraph from his hand.

JONAH ALEXANDER stop **HAYDEN WELLS** stop **BADLY WOUNDED.** stop **JEFFERSON BARRACKS HOSPITAL-** stop **DO MY BEST** stop **DOC**

Clay wanted to cry. Jonah didn't deserve this, and what was Hayden doing there? He wondered if Hayden shot Jonah, and then Jonah shot him. How was he going to tell Sunny that her worst nightmare had come true?

At least Jefferson Barracks wasn't that far away. Formerly a military post on the west bank of the Mississippi river, it had been turned into a hospital. It was only about 12 miles from St. Louis. The hospital boats often stopped there and brought wounded from the battlefields. It held over 2500 patients and kept doctors and nurses busy. Many men never left. North and South alike were buried on the grounds.

"You can't go all the way there by yourself. Be reasonable, Sunny, for Pete's sake." Clay said, exasperated.

"I'm going no matter what," Sunny said, her jaw set with determination.

"You just hold on. I know you're going but you just give me a little time and let me figure out what to do. We need to talk to your father, and we will work it all out. What good will you do Jonah if you get killed by some of Quantrill's band of cutthroats?"

"Okay, I will pack a few things and wait for you to get back to me, but you had better have a solution by morning," she said, leaving no doubt that she meant it.

"I will be ready by morning." Clay pulled his hat down on his head. He was as upset as Sunny, but he knew they needed to plan this expedition, not just run headlong into it.

"I'm puzzled about Hayden and him both being wounded. Makes me think there was some sort of confrontation. I know Hayden wouldn't have a chance in a shootout. It's sure got me puzzled," Clay said.

"Do you think Hayden shot him in the back or something?" Sunny asked, worry lines etching her face.

"We won't know anything until we get there, and maybe not then. Depends on what shape they're in."

"Please hurry, Clay. I'm worried. I want to get there as soon as possible," she said, with tears in her eyes. Fear gripped her. "Hurry Clay,"

"I'm on my way"

Sunny collapsed into the nearest chair and began to sob. Molly, who had been standing by, dropped to her knees and gathered her in her arms. She knew how she felt.

"Oh, Molly, what can I do even when I get there? I know Doc is doing his best, all I can do is pray and worry," she said, tears still rolling down her face.

Clay, Ian, and Isaiah, all planned to go. They decided that Sunny should dress as a young boy again. They didn't trust the fact that a young woman would be safe on the road. Isaiah tried to talk her out of going, but she wouldn't hear of it. Ian suggested they take Mr. Hodge's undertaker wagon. Nobody would be much interested in the dead. They decided to put a coffin in the back and if need be Sunny could hide in it until danger was over. Isaiah would drive and Ian and Clay would ride with their shotguns, watching for trouble.

Sunny was in a state of turmoil. If they had no trouble it was going to take them four to five days to get there. She felt like she was going to dissolve into hysterics. She knew that was not going to help. Her dad and the guys would do their best. All she could do was pray, and wait.

The first couple of days went well. The German Militia kept St. Jo safe, plus the Union army was near, but the farther south they went, the bigger chance of trouble. As they traveled, Sunny noticed the men were all very attentive to their surroundings.

"Some riders are coming. Get in the back Sunny." She rolled off the seat in a flash and got into the coffin. How eerie it was. She wanted to leave the top up, but knew that wouldn't do any good if they looked, so she took the scarf from around her neck and folded it at the edge of the top, so some air could come in and she could hear. It wouldn't be enough to notice, if someone just looked. Playing really dead would be the hardest part if they opened it up.

She heard the riders come to a halt by the wagon as it stopped.

"Good day gents. Where are you headed with this meat wagon?"

"We are going to Jefferson Barracks to pick up a young son for one of our friends. They want his body brought back," Isaiah stated.

"I'm the sheriff in St. Joseph. We are all friends of the family."

"We kind of guard this area. We live a few miles away and shoot off signals to our neighbors if we see any danger," the man explained.

"I'm just a sheriff. I just keep the law. It has nothing to do with the war."

"Well, I guess you can't do much damage. Three men. Go on and get your corpse."

They rode off in the opposite direction without another word. Sunny was shaking. Just their voices scared her. She was glad she hadn't seen their faces.

Each night they pulled the wagon into the safest area they could find and took turns sleeping while two watched and kept the campfire going. There wasn't room in the wagon with the coffin taking up so much space, but it helped keep out the cold. As soon as daylight appeared they were traveling again. They finished their journey without any more incidents.

When they were a few hours ride from their destination, Sunny put on a clean dress, washed the grime from her face and combed her hair. Anxiety was racing through her body. Oh soon, Jonah, I will be there soon. Hold on.

As they approached Jefferson Barracks, named for Thomas Jefferson, it was apparent that it was once a military post. It once served the new settlers and kept hostile Indians at bay. Soldiers had been there through every conflict since it had been built in 1831. Docked, not far away on the Mississippi, was a hospital ship. In 1862 they needed a hospital more than an outpost. It had long rows of buildings, one and two stories high and a porch with big columns on three sides, shaded with trees. The open end faced toward the river. On a bluff, a flagpole stood with a American flag blowing in the breeze. Several hundred yards back from the river stood a chapel. New buildings had been built and stood in rows and were one story high and about 600 feet long.

When they entered the barracks they saw massive dining rooms. People were at the tables, although it was about dark and supper seemed to be over.

"I will talk to someone and see where we can go," Clay said, as he headed toward a woman wiping a table. As he talked to the lady, Sunny noticed some of the men wore bandages. They looked like they were healing and were having coffee and talking to each other. Clay returned and said there was a desk down the hallway. They were soon directed to the new area on the west side of the main building. Sunny couldn't slow down. She was half walking and half running. When they entered the building, a receptionist told them that Jonah was in a ward not far from where they were standing.

After looking at a few beds, she spotted him lying in bed, not moving. She ran over to him, sat on the side of the bed, and laid her hand on his bare arm.

"Jonah, can you hear me. I love you." She pulled the covers low and saw his chest was bandaged. She listened to his raspy breathing. "Oh, Jonah," she said as she laid her head on his arm and began to weep. She felt her dad walk up behind her and lay his hands on her shoulders.

"He's strong Sunny. Have faith," her father said, swallowing a lump in his own throat. Sunny had held on so long believing that she and Jonah could work everything out. Isaiah whispered a prayer "Oh Lord, I can't believe that Jonah is going to die now. Please give him back to my daughter. She loves him deeply. I will always accept your will in our lives, but I pray for his life now. Please heal him."

"I will go look for someone who knows about his condition," Clay said, as he headed out the door.

"Maybe Doc's around," Ian said. "I only met him once, but I've heard a lot about him," he said, as he paced the floor by Jonah's bed looking at some of the other men. Most of them looked pretty bad with bandages wrapped around their heads or arms.

"That would be good if he was around. He could give us some answers for sure," Isaiah said.

Clay returned following a nurse after a short time.

"Hello, Mrs. Alexander. I am Mrs. Nichols. I am a volunteer nurse here. Sheriff Myers told me you were here. I know you're worried, but we are keeping him asleep right now. He has a serious wound in his chest, but he looks worse than he is," she said, as she leaned closer to Sunny. "I am not trying to say that he can get up tomorrow, but he is a strong man and he has been awake from time to time, but he is in quite a bit of pain. We don't want him to break his stitches loose and cause some internal bleeding so the doctor is keeping him under."

"Thank you, Mrs. Nichols," Sunny said, as tears rolled down her cheek. "Is Doc Egan around anywhere?"

"He should be making his rounds in the next hour or so. He snatches a bit of sleep from time to time. But your husband is his patient so he will be coming in here. If there is anything I can do for you, let me know, she said.

"Thank you," Sunny replied.

"If any of you want some coffee, just go to the dining room. I need to get back to my work now. Don't worry, Mrs. Alexander, it will take time, but he will be well one day," she said, as she turned to leave.

"Jonah's lucky. I guess Hayden isn't doing as well," Clay announced. "Mrs. Nichols said it's still not known if he will walk when he does heal.

"Did she say what happened?" Isaiah asked.

"Evidently Jonah was helping Hayden. He found him wounded on the battlefield, even though he was dressed in gray. Nothing like we thought."

"Oh, Jonah. How proud I am of you," Sunny whispered as she kissed the side of his face.

"Doc's coming!" Clay said, turning to Sunny. "Maybe he will be able to set our minds at ease."

"Well, hello there Clay, Isaiah," Doc said, as he walked past them and made his way to Sunny.

"He's going to make it, girl. Don't worry. Jonah is strong. He lost a lot of blood and was in a lot of pain, but he was lucky. There was no lasting damage to any vital organs. He will be as good as new when he heals. I am giving him some morphine for the pain, but it will wear off soon and he will wake up. He thrashes around too much when he's awake, and I want him to be still." Doc leaned over and patted Sunny's shoulder. "Don't you worry none. We are taking good care of him."

"Thank you! I'm so glad you were here" Sunny exclaimed, looking at Doc with relief.

"Aren't you the young fellow that's runnin' Jonah's smithy," Doc said, as he looked over at Ian. "I think I met you once when I came home for a couple of days."

"Yes, I am Ian. I met you right before Jonah left. I'm surprised you remembered me from that one short meeting."

"I'm pretty good with faces, but names take me a while."

"Why don't I try and find you people a bed for the night" Doc said, to the tired looking group. "The parson and his wife have a few beds in their spare room."

"That's okay. We brought some bedding and we have a wagon," Clay answered, rolling his shoulders, ready to go to bed anywhere.

"It's cold out tonight. I'll send someone over to arrange you all for the night. They put people up all the time."

"I'm not going anywhere," Sunny said, matter-of-factly.

"Okay, after I check Jonah, I will get you a chair to set beside his bed. Once he wakes up and you see that he's okay, you can go bunk down on one of the nurse's cots."

After everyone left and Doc had a chair brought in for her, she pulled it up close and laid her head on the bed beside Jonah, still holding his arm, and swiftly fell asleep.

Pain gripped at Jonah's chest. It didn't seem quite as bad as the last time he woke, but bad enough to let him know he was still alive. He felt something soft against his side. He slowly opened his eyes and turned his head to look. "*Sunny.*" He should have known. She never gave up on him. She fought for them against all odds.

He hadn't believed there was any chance that a woman like her would ever love anyone like him, but she had. No one had ever loved him before this. It was a new experience, one he was addicted to. He never wanted to live without her.

She must have traveled across some dangerous territory to get to him. How did she do it? It sent fear zinging through him just thinking about her putting herself

149

in such danger. There could have been Confederate soldiers anywhere out there, or even worse, Quantrill's band of raiders.

He tried to lift his hand to touch her hair and realized she had a grip on his wrist. He didn't want to disturb her, but he wanted to touch her. It had been so long since he had held her. He didn't even remember how many months since he had been gone. One had run into another until it seemed like an eternity. The memory of her was all that kept him warm. Sometimes he thought it was just a dream, a vision of his imagination, but here she was.

"Sunny" he said softly. "Sunny." She raised her head and he saw the love in her blue eyes. She leaned over him and kissed his lips and ran her hand through his hair.

"Jonah, you're awake," she said as tears sprang into her eyes. "I have been waiting hours for you to wake up. How do you feel?"

"Why do you love me so much?" he asked. "I will never understand how I got such a gift as you."

"You don't understand, but I got a gift when I got you too."

"I hope you never change your mind."

"I won't," she said, smiling. "Do you want me to get Doc? Are you hurting?"

"No, I just want to touch you."

She smiled as she took his hands in hers and laid her cheek against his whiskered and rough one. She whispered into his ear, "I love you Jonah Alexander, my husband, my friend, my hero."

Sunny stayed at Jefferson Barracks. Her father, Clay and Ian returned to St. Jo. Doc arranged for her to sleep in the nurse's quarters. She stayed by Jonah's side until she knew he was well. She began helping the nurses out doing small jobs around Jonah's ward. Soon Jonah was moved to another ward where the men recovering were not as critical. They visited with the men there and she even wrote some letters for them.

There were young boys without arms or legs. She knew how hard life was going to be for them. Jonah was regaining his strength little by little. They found out from Doc that Hayden was doing better, but he never gave them any details. One day a nurse told her that he was sitting up but he couldn't move his legs yet, so they didn't know if he would walk again or not. Jonah and she prayed for Hayden to recover. He had given them many problems, but he was just a young man with some misguided ideas.

The November day pleased them. Sunlight shone outside almost like a spring day. Sunny was sitting with her husband in the dining room. He walked the halls now, to get his strength back. Jonah sat at the table, away from his dreaded bed. He still needed it, not being well enough yet.

"I wish the war was over and you were home. We would go riding, plant a garden, and take walks," she said, wistfully

"Me too, sweetheart. Nothing sounds better than that," he said, holding her hands in his.

"Are you going back to the war when you get well?" she asked, looking at him waiting for his answer.

"You know I have to. I only went for Simon and I have to finish it for Simon. Wherever he is, if he is still alive, I have to fight so he can be a free man someday"

"I know. You're that kind of man, and as bad as I hate you going back, I knew that's how you would feel."

"Should we walk back to that cursed bed? I have never been knocked on my feet before like this. I guess I thought when the wound healed you could just get up and go."

"It takes time Jonah. You were wounded badly. Hang on, it won't be long."

Three weeks later Doc escorted them home aboard a hospital ship. Clay and Isaiah picked them up at the dock and took them home. They were both so glad to finally make it back. Jonah could heal there.

Jonah tried to get Sunny to stay at Molly's so people wouldn't know they were married. He still didn't trust that someone wouldn't harm her if they knew she was married to a half-breed. He wasn't in any shape to take care of her yet. Sunny refused. She told him it was time people knew and she would handle any problem that arrived. Jonah had been here for years, and most people had accepted him as he was. She knew feelings ran deep with the war, especially since Missouri was so split on slavery. It didn't matter. She wanted to live with her husband openly. People respected her father, and many attended his church. Most of the men were in the war, and so mostly women were involved, and she knew she could handle them.

Sunny's parents announced in the St. Jo paper that Jonah had been wounded. He was home to heal, and his wife Sarah was by his side.

Questions started circulating, but with Sunny's parents, Clay, Ian, and Molly, telling everyone when they got married, soon everyone knew the whole story. Some even dropped by to see how Jonah was and visited with Sunny. She almost always had to explain that they married when Jonah was on leave and they wanted time together before he left again.

Jonah got stronger each day, and Sunny both loved and dreaded it. She knew when he was well that he would have to go back to the war, which was still in full force. Young men were being killed by the thousands and she feared that she could still end up losing him. She wanted to hide with him in some distant land, so he could stay with her. She prayed constantly that God would keep him safe.

Jonah snuck walks outdoors to run in the hills when Sunny was out of the house. The first time he went she protested that he wasn't well enough yet to exert himself that much, but Jonah knew he would never get well if he didn't build his body back up. He had just returned from a walk up the hill outside of his place, and was sitting at the table getting his breath back. He felt as weak as a newborn kitten. Jonah knew the minute Sunny came in that she was upset. She put her few items that she had picked up, and came over and hugged him. She didn't ask how he was feeling, something she did several times a day. She was like a little mother hen. She chatted about how sugar was getting hard to find lately while putting her things away. Jonah knew she wasn't upset with him, because she had never been shy about letting him know. No, this was something else.

"Come here and sit down," Jonah said, as he held out his hand to her. Sunny walked over slowly, took his hand and sat in the chair that he had pulled over next to him.

"What's going on?"

"Nothing important," she said, as she shrugged her shoulders.

"I know you are upset. Is it anything I did?"

"Oh no, Jonah. I'm not upset with you," she said, as she looked at him with her frank blue eyes."

"Tell me. I thought we were supposed to share everything," he said, softly.

"It's that hateful Mrs. Baggs. She is such an old sour lady, so full of hateful ideas."

"It was about you marrying me, wasn't it?"

"Yes, but I don't care what she thinks. I feel sorry for her husband and children."

"We were expecting this, weren't we?" he said, softly.

"Yes, it's the reason you wouldn't marry me for so long," she said, smiling. "But I finally convinced you in the end, didn't I?"

"I still think it would have been best for you if I had stuck to my guns, but I just can't make myself let you go. My heart overrides my good sense."

"Oh, Jonah, it's not all that bad. I'm just spoiled. All my life people have liked me, and this mean spirited lady said such foul. nasty things to me."

"Just walk away, Sweetheart. That's the best thing you can do."

"Oh, I walked away, after I told her what I thought," Sunny explained, with a mischievous grin on her face.

"Don't tell me."

"Okay, I won't," she commented.

"What did you say to her?"

"I told her that I would forgive her for being such a narrow-minded bigot. I told her God probably wouldn't though, because He knew that my husband was a much better person than she would ever be. I told her she wouldn't know a good man if he was right in front of her busybody nose, that Mr. Baggs was probably a decent fellow until the likes of her snagged him. Then I stuck my nose in the air and told her I would forgive her, because I sure didn't want to be like her, and walked around her without looking back."

"Come here," he said as he pulled her into his arms. "You don't have to defend me, sweetheart. It's mild compared to what I have heard in my lifetime."

"I will always defend you. Isn't it awful that we have to fight a war over a person's place in life? People actually believe that they have a right to own another human being, or if they aren't allowed to own them, then a right to degrade them. It's awful Jonah, and it makes me so mad that you have to fight a war to have the freedom you should rightfully have. People need to give Simon the right to be free. It's not fair."

"Are you not the same beautiful lady that taught me that life isn't fair and that we just hang on and keep our faith?"

Sunny looked up at him, and smiled. "I did, didn't I, and I didn't think you believed me."

"I believe you and you're going to have to forgive her. She might end up being one of the nicer people in our lives," he said, seriously.

"We can handle it," she stated, as she put her arms around the only man she had ever loved.

♥

Chapter 19

Jonah almost recovered completely. He spent many days down at the smithy swinging the hammer and managing the forge. Sunny knew it wouldn't be long until he returned to the war. She dreaded every day knowing that soon he would inform her it was time to go back. She decided to see Molly while Jonah was with Ian. As she walked along the street she noticed, as always, the few people about town that seemed to cross the street before she got to them. She noticed it more and more, but she didn't mention it to anyone. She was sure that Jonah probably was treated the same, but he was so used to it, she wondered if he noticed. He didn't seem to waste time on things like that, or at least he didn't show it. It hurt Sunny's feelings and she knew that's what Jonah had tried to tell her before they got married. It didn't matter. Those people would never be as important to her as he was. Molly must have seen her coming when she met her at the door.

"Come in. I just made some lemonade, I'll fix us a glass and we will sit on the back porch," she said as she went into the kitchen. Sunny followed her and they carried their refreshment out to the porch and sat down.

"Where's little Mack? He usually greets me with wet kisses," Sunny asked.

"He wore himself out and fell asleep right after lunch. He never slows down," Molly said, smiling with pride. "Is Jonah still spending his days helping Ian?"

"Yes, he's determined to get well, and he's almost as good as new."

"You don't exactly seem pleased," Molly said, as she looked at her best friend.

"Of course I want him well, but I just dread the time when he goes back to this awful war. I thought it would be over with by now," she answered, exasperated.

"I understand how you feel. When Mack decided to go at the very first, I couldn't believe that he would leave me and our little son. I didn't think he would die or that it would be so bad. Losing him was so hard," she said, sadly.

"He has been gone almost a year now. I know how hard it was for you. I was with you during that time. Does it still bother you, Molly?"

"Sunny, I am so confused. I loved Mack, but Ian has come to mean so much to me. I didn't think I would ever love again, but I am feeling things for him that I probably shouldn't. Little Mack is crazy about him. I am a lot more mature now than when I fell in love with Mack. Ian never says anything, so I'm not sure how he feels."

"Molly, Ian has loved you since he met you."

"How do you know that?" Molly asked as she looked keenly at Sunny.

"When Mack died I found Ian in great despair. He hated himself for loving you when you had a husband. He was riddled with guilt. I told him his feelings for you had nothing to do with it. He decided he would just be your friend. He loves you Molly, but I don't think the guilt he carries will ever let him tell you his true feelings. You will have to drag it out of him. I think he would give up his own life to bring Mack back to you."

Molly covered her face with her hands and began to sob. Sunny moved over and gathered her in her arms.

"Molly, what is it? What's wrong?"

"That's so touching. I do love him, Sunny. He is such a good man, and so unselfish," she said, wiping her eyes.

"So do something about it. Life is too short to pass up. Tell him how you feel, and make him a happy man."

"I'm not a very forward person. I'm not sure how to go about it."

"You will find a way Molly. I practically threw myself at Jonah. He wanted no part of me."

"Only because he was afraid of how people would treat you."

"He was right on that score. We have been snubbed by the best of them lately."

"Have you really?" Molly asked, surprised.

"Don't tell me you haven't noticed?"

"I haven't. I am really surprised. Jonah is a good man."

"That doesn't matter to some people. He's half Indian and therefore he's to be looked down on."

"Who treats you like that?"

"Mrs. Baggs, Mrs. Newman and her daughter, Susanna and that family that lives out by the Fultz's."

"You mean Mr. and Mrs. Everhart. They are all friends. I imagine that they are just following Mrs. Baggs' lead. I don't think they really feel that way about Jonah," Molly explained.

"After the war, Jonah and I are moving to Denver City. We both think people that are settling new lands have more on their minds than to look down on their neighbors."

"Does it really bother you that much?"

"No, I could put up with it, but we don't want to raise our children in that kind of environment. We want them to feel loved and liked by other children." Sunny said, as she took another sip of her lemonade.

"I can't stand the thought of you leaving again, Sunny. You're my best friend."

"I know, and you're mine, but we feel like it's a move we need to make. In fact." Sunny stopped in mid-sentence. She didn't know if she should tell Molly her secret yet.

"In fact what?" Molly asked, looking at Sunny for an answer.

"I am going to have a baby," she replied, smiling.

"Oh Sunny, that's great news," she said, excitedly.

"I haven't told Jonah yet."

"Why ever not?" she said, wrinkling her brow, not understanding her friend at all.

"Jonah would send me to Denver City when he returned to the war. It was a bargain we made when we got married."

"You're not thinking of not telling him, are you?"

"I really considered it, but I thought maybe that knowledge might keep him going. If he thought about seeing his child, it just might be the thing he needs. But if

I'm so far away and if anything happened like it did, it would take me forever to get to him."

"Oh, Sunny, you have to tell him. You would not like him to keep something so important from you. Besides, a promise is a promise."

"I know I will have to tell him, but I am dreading what he will say."

Jonah was well and she knew it wouldn't be long until he returned to his unit. Sunny knew, as bad as she hated it, she was going to have to let him go. She had put off telling him about the baby and she knew it was time that she did. They always sat on the porch at night and watched the sunset, and most of the time stayed there into the evening. She finished up the supper dishes as Jonah came in from his walk after feeding the horses. He poured a cup of coffee, still warm on the stove, and took a seat at the table. "I have decided to go back to my unit next week," he announced, looking at her as she was drying the last of the dishes.

"You can't do that!" she exclaimed, turning around to face him.

"You know that I am well. I would love to stay here forever and forget about the war, but I can't," he said, looking at her with a deep sadness in his eyes. Sunny knew that he hated to go as much as she hated for him to go.

"Come here," he said, reaching for her hand and pulling her down onto his lap. He held her against him and neither one of them said anything for a few minutes. "I will be back as soon as I can. You know that. If this war would end I would hightail it back here so fast that they would wonder what happened to me."

"I know," she said.

"Jonah, I have put off telling you something important," she added.

After a short hesitation, he said, "Okay, tell me now."

"I'm going to have a baby," she said so softly, that Jonah wasn't sure he heard her right. He raised her chin up, so he could look into her eyes.

"You're going to have a baby?" he asked, trying to hide the fear in his eyes. "Why did you wait to tell me?"

"You know why. Because I promised to go away if that happened, and I don't want to be that far away from you."

"Sunny, if you were right beside me, there wouldn't be a thing you could do."

"I could pray."

"You can do that anyway."

"I know, and I do trust God, but I saw when they brought Mack home and how torn up Molly was. Jonah, I would die if something happened to you."

"How do you think I would feel if someone hurt you and the baby? Do you really want to risk our baby's life for so little of a reason?"

"Of course not. Do you really think it will be any better in Denver City?"

"I do. The farther west you go, the more diverse the people are, and their only concern is farming their land, working their trap lines, or whatever else they are doing to make a way in life. Less of this war is touching them."

"Fine, I will go if that's what you want me to do. My parents have promised to go with me. I will have to tell them, and we will make arrangements to go in the next few weeks. Don't you hate leaving all your friends and the business that you have built from the ground up?" she asked.

"Yes, but our family is more important. Your safety is more important. Life is tough sometimes."

"You know all about that, don't you?" she asked, looking at him with admiration in her eyes. Sunny knew her life had been easy up until now. She supposed it was time for her to build a deep character, like her husband. She would do what he asked of her, if it would keep his mind worry free. At least her parents would be with her, and she

159

couldn't ask for more. She would wait out the war until he came back to her.

"Promise me you will go. I will make arrangements with Ian to escort you back there. We can get someone to take care of the smithy while he is gone."

"I will go, Jonah, I promise."

Jonah worked very hard getting a wagon ready to go on the trip. After making arrangements with Ian he talked to Isaiah, making him promise to take her. He designed a well hidden space under the wagon to put their money, and showed Sunny and Isaiah where it was. He didn't want them to worry about cash, and didn't want anyone to find it on them. The night before Jonah went back, they hardly slept, knowing this would be the last night together until the war was over. They hoped that would be soon. Jonah hadn't left as soon as he had planned. He wanted to see them packed and ready to travel, but the days dragged along because Isaiah had to make plans before he left the church, and friends had to say goodbye.

He waited until everybody was ready to go before he left. Molly was there to see Ian off, as well as Sunny and her parents. Most of the church ladies were there to see Isaiah and Bess off. Jonah had to keep kissing his wife before they finally waved goodbye and rolled out of town. Sunny waved to him until she was out of sight. He knew she was crying, and he felt like it too. He should be with her, and he promised himself if he made it back and they were together again, nothing in this world would keep them apart.

"Are you sure this is the right thing to do, old friend?" Clay said, as he walked up to Jonah, just as he started to mount his horse.

"As sure as I can be for a dumb Indian."

"I think you could have made it here. You have been here for a long time, and you have friends to stand behind you."

"I know, Clay, and I will always appreciate your friendship. I would have liked to stay here. It's been my home for a long time, the only one I have ever known. But Sunny and the baby are my home now. I have to do what's right by them, and this just seems right. I don't think when the war is over, that it will really be over. There will be many hard feelings between the different sides for a long time." Jonah leaned on his horse and dropped his head. "If I made the wrong decision, and something happens to Sunny and our baby, I will always hate myself, but if she stayed here and something happened, I would hate myself too. I just hope I'm doing the right thing."

"I hope you will be back soon, and don't worry about Sunny. Isaiah took care of her for many years, and I'm sure he will take good care of her now."

"That's what I'm countin' on."

"You be careful," Clay said, as he reached over and gave his friend a big bear hug and slapped him on the back."

"So long Clay. I'll see you when I get back." Jonah said, as he swung into the saddle, crammed his hat down over his eyes, and rode away from his life. Clay watched him go until he was out of sight, and said a prayer for his best friend.

Jonah told Sunny that it would take a while to get to Denver City because it was over 600 miles. It took them a little more than a month. Most of the soldiers in Denver City stayed there to fight Indians. Tribal wars were on the rise because the Indians felt threatened by so many newcomers that had invaded the country because of the gold rush in 1861. Denver City now had a population of almost 5,000 people. There was talk of making it Colorado territory instead of belonging to Kansas, as it did now.

When they got into town they stopped at the Denver City mercantile to get supplies before they found their place. They looked around the large store. It had everything from food to mining supplies, and whatever you might want in between. After picking out food supplies, Isaiah asked the lady behind the counter how long she had lived there.

"I came here three years ago. In fact I was a mail order bride," she said proudly.

"It looks like it worked out," he said, smiling.

"Yes, it did for us. There were a lot of mail order brides at that time, but some worked out and some didn't. We have several ladies that were abandoned here. I feel very lucky. My name is Rosie Dunn, and my husband is the proprietor, Andrew Dunn. Are you moving here?" she asked.

"Yes, my daughter's husband is in the war, and her grandfather gave her some land that he owned here. In fact, we wondered if you might direct us to Arnold Snead's property, west of the city."

"I will call my husband. He might know," she said, as she stepped through a door and talked to someone.

Sunny thought the woman looked in her late twenties. Her husband walked into the room. He looked close to forty, tall, and tough, until she looked into his twinkling blue eyes.

"I hear you are looking for the Snead property?"

"Yes, my father-in-law gave my daughter some property outside of the city. It's supposed to be prime grazing land and someone was to build a cabin, Isaiah said, as he shook the man's hand.

"I can direct you. It is about three miles west right after you cross over the bridge of Cherry creek. The property is right along the banks of the creek and Met Baughman, a big Norwegian built a fine log house there. He was hired by your father-in-law. Met is your closest neighbor and a good one to have. If you need anything just call on him. Me and Rosie want to welcome you to Denver City. It's in its youth but has grown out of a mining town, and we hope it goes places someday. My Rosie and I will help any way we can. You just call on us."

They followed the directions that the Dunn's had given them, and after crossing the bridge they saw a log house sitting down a lane lined by fencing. It was beautiful land, lush and green with a giant oak tree standing over the house. Sunny got tears in her eyes. Her grandfather had given her a great gift. She just hoped that Jonah would soon be home to share it with her.

Sunny and her parents were glad to call a place home after so long on the trail. She wanted to wash the grit and grime from her body, but knew that they had to unhitch the horses and unload the wagon before they did anything. The house was spacious and clean. Her neighbor had done a wonderful job on it. There was a large parlor with a big fireplace and kitchen. In time she would have a wood stove for cooking and a table to take meals from. She discovered, after more exploring that there were two bedrooms and a loft, plenty of sleeping room, even for a growing family. She pressed her hand to her stomach, knowing in a few months that she would have Jonah's child. She hoped this was a good place to raise their children. She silently sent up a prayer that God would bring Jonah safely home.

They washed up and had leftover bread and beans from their last meal on the trail. Everyone was so tired from traveling that they went to sleep in their beds, the only furniture they brought with them. Sunny fell asleep the minute her head hit the pillow. The last thing she remembered hearing was the tumbling waters of the creek, running close to the house, the chirping of crickets, and croaking of frogs.

Sunny and her father walked along the creek, discovering things about their new home. She found some blackberry bushes and hickory nut trees.

"I believe that is a cherry tree there," Isaiah said, pointing to a tree on the other side of the creek.

"That looks like green fruit on it. It won't be long until they are ripe," she replied, smiling.

"You might have to fight the birds for them."

"Drat! And the squirrels for the nuts. I just ask that they leave me my share," she said with a giggle.

"I think that might be your neighbor coming. He is a big man, for sure." Isaiah noted. The man rode up to where they were walking. He was tall, broad shouldered, and stocky built. He looked middle aged, with graying brown hair. He exerted so little effort dismounting his horse that he looked like he just stepped from it.

"I'm assuming you'd be Mrs. Alexander," he said with a slight accent. The first thing Sunny noticed was his big friendly smile. She knew this was a man who could be a friend, but with his size, only a fool would want to tangle with him.

"Yes, I'm Mrs. Alexander, please call me Sunny. And this is my father, Isaiah Markley," she said, reaching to shake his hand.

"Glad to finally meet you. I just finished the house a couple of weeks ago. The barn needs more work, but I hope it's okay until I can finish it."

"It's fine, Mr. Baughman," she answered, smiling.

"Call me Met. My wife will be over in a couple of days to meet you. She never gets in a big hurry. She says you need to rest awhile before people barge in on you. Not like me," he explained, giving a big laugh.

Sunny liked her new neighbor a lot. He was polite, yet had a familiar way about him, making him easy to get to know.

Two days later, just like he said, his wife came with him to call. She was of Indian decent. Sunny's heart thrilled. If nobody else in this town would accept them, these people would. She became fast friends with the couple. Robin was half Indian. Her father had been an Irish fur trapper and she knew Indian customs and languages along with Irish ones. She had married Met at seventeen when he first came to the country. Sunny was happy to have some friends until Jonah came home.

Over the next couple of months Sunny got the things she needed for her house. Robin came to visit and help. They sat together and had long conversations. Robin took Bess and Sunny to town in their wagon. She learned that there were several things in town that she didn't expect, like a library, newspaper, doctor, and a hat shop. Robin pointed out the church, and told Bess that Isaiah should meet the pastor, for he was getting on in years and would probably welcome some help. Sunny was amazed how many people Robin knew and associated with. She dressed differently from the other women, with brightly colored clothes and a long braid that swung down her back. She made no secret that she was part Indian.

It didn't take her father long to acquaint himself with the church pastor and was soon performing the night services. Sunny and her parents became known around town and met more people. Sunny just wished the war was over and Jonah was home.

Sunny and Bess put up the last of the garden vegetables. Sunny was only two months away from having her baby, and still the war wasn't over. She hoped that Jonah would be home before the baby was born. She rarely got a letter. Her father went to town most days and always checked the post office, but they were far and few between. She knew they just didn't get to her like they should, and wondered if Jonah got hers.

"Sit down and rest, Sunny. I don't need your help. Sit, child," Bess said, as she stopped and guided Sunny to the rocking chair.

"I just feel so miserable, Mom. Is this normal?" she asked, looking at her mom with concern.

"Of course it is, Sweetie. The baby is just taking all your energy."

"Mom, I seem to be so emotional lately. Sometimes I cry myself to sleep. I want Jonah home. I have been writing him the most whining letters lately and I know I shouldn't. He has enough to concern himself about without worrying about me."

"That's normal, Sunny. Jonah understands that you miss him. He's probably happy to know you miss him so much."

"I miss Molly, Ian, and little Mack. Does it ever strike you that we might never see them again? Isn't it sad?"

"Are you homesick?"

"I think so. I really like Robin, Met, the Dunn's, and all the other new friends, but I love my old friends too."

"Sunny, I am afraid that is life. You just have to be thankful that they were part of yours. Move on and never forget them."

"How did you do it, Mom, moving so often from place to place to follow Papa where God led him? "

"No matter who you meet or where you live, you are just happy that you're with your family. You will feel differently when Jonah gets home. It will make a great deal of difference when he is beside you every day." Sunny wanted him to hurry, and she knew she wasn't the only wife of a soldier that felt that way. She also knew that many husbands and sons would not return home after the war. It was so sad. She selfishly prayed it wouldn't be her situation.

When September just had days to go before October arrived, Sunny gave birth to her baby girl. She hoped that Jonah would be back by then, but he didn't make it to see his daughter come into the world. She looked so much like Jonah, with her dark curls, and coffee and cream skin. Sunny loved her daughter instantly. She was her father's child. She knew that Jonah would have preferred her to be whiter looking, so she would have no troubles in life, but Sunny was pleased that she bore his trademark. She hoped that her daughter would have the pride and grit that Robin had. As she held her baby in her arms and looked into her tiny and perfect face, she noticed that she had her blue eyes. "I see that you have some of your mother's marking too," she said. "We'll see if you keep them."

"May I see my brand new granddaughter?" Isaiah said, as he poked his head into the room.

"Of course, Papa, come on in."

Isaiah walked into the room and bent over his granddaughter. He picked up her tiny hand and stroked it with his thumb. He felt like his heart was in his throat. This child was special. Bess and he had been here through the whole process, taking Jonah's place while he was away at war. He loved his grandson, but Levi and Mary were always with him, and he would never have the same problems that this little girl would have. He just prayed that Jonah had made a good decision moving them here.

"What a beautiful child you have, Sunny," he said, still holding her hand and looking her over.

"Oh, Papa, she is beautiful. She looks like her father," she said, smiling.

"I'm sure as she grows she will develop some more traits that you will recognize as your own. She is a blending of two different people, and will develop into her own person someday."

"Jonah should be home. It's unfair that he misses this time."

"He will be here for any more that you will have."

"For sure. Mom and Robin were wonderful. They helped me through it all."

"Yes, they did good. They are patting themselves on the back for their part in this little one's entry into this world. What are you going to name her?"

"Johanna Bess, after Jonah and Mom. What do you think? We could call her Jo or Hannah or even just Anna."

"That's perfect," he said, as he kissed his daughter on the forehead.

Little Hannah, with all the love she received from her mother and grandparents, grew and flourished. Her hair took on a lighter hue than her father's, but still left no doubt that she was very much like him, except for her blue eyes. Robin and Met were honored with the role of godparents, which made them very proud. They had never been able to have one of their own, and Sunny knew they would have made great parents.

Sunny was amazed at the winter in Denver. She had never seen so much snow. Met and Robin helped them gather and cut wood for the winter, and she couldn't believe that they needed so much. Sunny and her father had to dig a trail to the barn just to feed the horses and their one milk cow. They made a trail to the well and brought in water. If it had not been for Met and Robin they would have never been prepared for the cold. There had been snow in St. Jo, but never so much as here.

The snow piled up for weeks, and they celebrated Christmas by themselves, and still the war wasn't over. Met came through the snow on horseback every few days to check on them. When Sunny had decided they were buried in the house for the winter, a warm front came in and at the end of January the snow began to melt. She just got outside for awhile, when another spell of snowfall came. March brought in warm weather, and Sunny was ready for it. She walked around the grounds, enjoying the outdoors when her father came from town in the buggy. She met him at the barn, and he gave her a letter from Jonah. Sunny ripped it open in a hurry. She hadn't received a letter for ages. It was postmarked over a month ago. As she read his loving words to her, and tears gathered in her eyes, she wanted to drop to her knees in relief. She had worried for weeks that something had happened to him. She walked over to the fence, leaned on it, and reread each word again.

"Oh please bring him home soon,"

Baby Hannah was now six months old and growing like a weed. She crawled around the floor and played with small toys that Sunny and Bess made for her. She loved the noise of her best toys, tin cups and spoons. She was a happy child, and wasn't afraid of people. The baby would go to anyone with a little coaxing. Sunny rocked her to sleep at night and told her what it would be like when her father came home. Sunny hoped it would come true soon.

Sunny and Bess worked in their garden. They planted a big one, since they wanted many things to put up before winter. If another winter came like last year, they wanted to have plenty of rations.

Baby Hannah sat on a blanket, but Sunny had to put her back because she kept crawling off into the dirt. Finally she decided to let her go ahead and clean her up later. Hannah sifted the dirt with her hands and soon had it in her hair and all over her face. Sunny decided she had better take her into the house, clean her up and lay her down for a nap.

Just as soon as she headed for the house she heard her father racing the buggy into the pathway to the barn.

168

Her father never drove like that. She stood in shock wondering what was wrong. He leapt from the buggy, yelling

"The war is over! The war is over," waving a newspaper over his head. Sunny and Bess ran toward him. He stopped and held the newspaper up so that they could see it." The Confederacy surrendered. The war is over." All three of them hugged each other and cried. Their prayers had finally been answered. Baby Hannah started to cry and Sunny realized they had scared her. She held her daughter to herself, crooning the good news to her, "Your daddy is coming home, sweetheart. Your daddy is coming home."

Clay looked up when the door of his office opened, and let out a breath of relief. There stood Jonah.

"It's about time you showed yourself. I was about to get worried." Clay said, as he hurried from his desk and threw his arms around his friend. "What took you so blasted long to get here? The war has been over for more than a month."

I was in Maryland when it ended. The troubles kept moving east and me with it."

"Sit down Jonah. You're a sight for sore eyes," he said as he moved back to his chair and Jonah sat down.

"I'm so happy this war is over. I have to admit, I'm tired. I rode hard to get here as fast as I could. I still have a ways to go to get to Denver City, but it seemed like home was a good place to rest," he said, as he removed his Yankee hat.

"I know it was rough Jonah. We were lucky here in St. Jo. We didn't get near the war that other places did."

"I never want to think about any of it again. I guess we did what Simon wanted, and set his people free."

"Oh, speaking of Simon, I have something for you," he said, as he opened a bottom drawer of his desk, and pulled out an envelope. "This came for you about three weeks ago. "From Simon. So we know he is alive."

"Clay, you couldn't have given me better news," he said, as he took the letter from Clay's hands." I looked for him everywhere I went," he said, as a big smile broke across his face.

Jonah ripped the letter open and read:

Dear Jonah,

It's been three years since I lost you. I've been a little bit of everywhere. During one of our travels I found my brother. Then we found the rest of my family. We got them into Ohio where they are now living, and are safe. Many families came from the south into safe territory. I am going back to Ohio to live with my folks. But first I wanted to thank you for raising me, and taking such good care of me. You were, and always will be a father to me. You taught me things that my family never had the right to learn. They need me now, and I know that you will be okay with that. I hope someday I can come and visit you .I will always write and give you news about me. I hope you write me back and let me know all about you. I hope you married Miss Sunny. She loves you.

Your adopted son,

Simon

"Is he okay?" Clay asked.

"Yeah, he's okay, alive and well. He found his family and has them in Ohio. He said lots of families are there. I heard they were swarming into the northern states. The main thing is that he is alive, and has a future of his own choosing. Up until this point he had no choice in anything. Now I can breathe a sigh of relief over him. I can concentrate on getting to Denver, and back to Sunny and my new baby girl."

"I sure can't blame you for your move, but you have been the best friend I've ever had, Jonah. I'm gonna miss you."

"You have been the best friend I've ever had, Clay but sometimes life makes choices for you," he said, as he pulled his hat off his head.

Clay thought Jonah looked about as tired as a man could get.

"When are you going on to Denver City?"

"I am going to rest for a day, then get a couple of good horses together to take with me. Someday I want a good string. I will have to take Gypsy with me or Sunny would never forgive me," he said, smiling.

"Don't you think you need a little more rest than that?"

"I want to get there as soon as possible. I want some real clothes. I'm through with these Yankee blues," he declared.

"Are you gonna notify Sunny that you're well and on your way?"

"I will send her a telegram before I leave."

After Jonah selected a couple of good horses including Gypsy, and said goodbye to Joseph, Doc, Ian, Molly, and Clay, he sent a telegram to his wife. He sold his home and business to Ian. Now he was ready to make a new home in a new land, with the woman he loved. It was time to ride out with no regrets. He would never forget the few friends he had here, but life went on. He did this many times in his life when he was young, but he had put down roots here, so it was harder. Sunny was waiting for him and that's what made it all worthwhile. He left St. Jo leading three horses. Not many more than he had come to St. Jo with many years ago.

♥

Chapter 20
May 1865

The war ended in April, and that was almost two months ago. Sunny was uneasy. Why wasn't Jonah home? If something was wrong he should have written a letter, but she had heard nothing. Sunny walked along the creek, thinking and worrying about Jonah. She wouldn't let herself think that something had happened to him. She just wouldn't. She knew Doc or Clay would have notified her. Clay was the answer. She would send him a telegram. If he knew anything he would get back to her and knowing Clay, if he didn't know he would do his best to find out. Once she made up her mind she took off for the house. She would get her father to go to town to send a message.

"You look like you have a purpose," Isaiah said, as she came hurrying up the steps onto the porch where he was sitting.

"I do, Papa. I want you to go into town and send a telegram to Clay. Ask him if he has heard anything about Jonah."

"I know you're anxious, Sunny, but those boys can't get home in a day," he said, as he took hold of her hand.

"Papa, it's been almost two months"

"Okay, I will do it if it will set your mind at ease."

"It will. Tell Clay to answer me right back, please."

"Okay, I'll go right now. Is there anything else you need while I'm there?" he asked as he got ready to step down from the porch.

"Check the post office for mail while you're there."

Sunny waited until her father hitched the buggy and drove out of sight. She knew it would seem like hours before he got back. She decided she would see if baby Hannah was awake. She needed to hold her. Sunny knew it would make her feel better.

"Oh, Jonah, please hurry home," she said with a lump in her throat.

Sunny heard her father come in and went to the door to meet him. "Did you send the telegram?"

"Didn't have to. One was waiting for you," he said as he handed her the telegram.

Sunny ripped it open, and read aloud; *Leaving St. Jo today–* stop*– I will get there soon–* stop*– Can't wait to hold you Love, Jonah.*

"Oh Papa, He's on his way. He's finally on his way."

*   *

Sunny went to the porch swing and sat down to brush her hair. It was barely daylight and she always wanted to get dressed and enjoy the morning a bit before Hannah woke. It was still a little cool here in late May. St. Jo was already full of warm days by now. She was finally getting used to the short summers and long winters of this country. She had been waiting in anticipation for June to come because Jonah should be here by then. She wished away every day waiting for his arrival.

She was so thankful the war was over and he had lived through it. Jonah had been through a lot of hardships in his life and she hoped the war would be the end of them. She knew she was the cause of them having to move here. Jonah would have put up with anything for himself, but for her he had to make things better. She missed her friends in St. Jo, but she had made new friends here so she had no complaints. She was accustomed to moving. They had followed her father from place to place opening new churches. One more move was worth them being together.

Sunny heard a horse whinny in a far off distance. She rose from her seat, still brushing her hair, and saw a lone rider coming down the lane leading to the house. It was early for a visitor. The rider was bringing three horses behind him. Maybe he was trying to sell them, or was lost. She laid the brush down and stepped off of the porch.

173

Something was familiar about the way he sat on his horse. The rider started to gallop then, took his hat off and waved it above his head. Sunny's heart dropped. Nobody but Jonah could have such black hair.

"Jonah! Oh, Jonah!" she yelled as picked up her skirt hem and started to run. She could hardly see where she was going for the tears falling from her eyes.

Jonah stopped, leapt from his horse and ran toward her.They met in the middle of the road, throwing themselves into each other's arms. They clung together without a word. They were home. No matter where they lived, they were home in each other's arms. She laid her head upon his chest and cried tears of joy. He rested his head on top of hers and let the tears fall. At long last they kissed each other tenderly; then looked at each other and smilcd through their tears.

They were interrupted by Isaiah and Bess walking up to them to welcome Jonah home. In Bess's arms she held the little daughter whom he had never seen. He held out his arms to her and she smiled, reaching to him, just like she knew who he was. Jonah walked to his new home with his baby daughter in one arm and his other around his wife. Home, he was finally home.

Epilogue

Jonah stepped off the porch where he had been sitting with Sunny enjoying the late summer sunset. It was time to call the kids in. They would stay out all night if he didn't round them up. "Hannah! Joseph! Jacob! Seth! It's time to come in for the night."

He walked out and leaned over the fence looking over his horses. He had a good line. He had been happy with the decision to bring his mares with him from St. Jo, ten years ago. He sold the finest horses in the territory. Since the railroad had expanded it was easy to ship horses in and out of Denver. He sure couldn't complain.

He raised beef cattle, and did a little blacksmithing on the side. Jonah had many occupations, but he had never been a farmer. With Met's help he managed that too.

Jonah had a wiry old hired hand, Abe, who could do just about anything. He looked out for Jonah's family as well as his land. He was like a grandpa to the kids. He had even helped deliver Joseph in the middle of a raging snowstorm. After living through that birth, Jonah had said there would be no more kids. But that had been easier said than done. In ten years they had four kids, three wild boys and Hannah.

"Papa" yelled Joseph. "We can't find Seth."

"You had better find him! Check at Abe's. He's always stalking him."

Hannah was ten, and thought she was grown. She loved bossing her little brothers around. One minute she could be a lady sewing and cooking, and the next minute she was like the boys, playing outside, doing everything they did. Joseph was eight and wasn't afraid of anything. He was a natural born horseman. Jacob was six, and seemed to be a little more into reading and writing than Joseph. He loved horses too, but didn't have the natural way with them that Joseph did. Little four-year old Seth thought he should be able to keep up with his brothers. All the kids showed their Indian blood, but not as prominent as Jonah. The children had their mother's good nature and love for people.

Jonah didn't know what love was until Sunny taught him how and gave him children. Such feelings filled his heart just looking at them all. He had gone for many years never knowing anything about love, and now he knew how blessed he was. He would die a slow death if anything ever happened to them.

With the railroad making it so easy to travel, they had been back to St. Jo and visited. Molly married Ian and they had two more children. People who had known Little Mack father commented on how much he looked like him, but as far as little Mack was concerned, Ian was his father and Ian felt the same way about his son. Clay was still the sheriff there, and would most likely be for a long time, but they kept in touch. Clay would have a special place in Jonah's heart, a friend who had always been there for him during the rough times. Simon, true to his word, always kept in touch with Jonah. He helped his family in Ohio. Jonah encouraged him to breed good horses; and with his experience as a blacksmith, he made a good living. He was now married and had a couple of little boys. Maybe the war would help those boys of Simon's and make a better world for all.

It took years to rebuild the war torn lands. Isaiah and Bess went back to St. Jo for awhile thinking they could help in some way. St. Jo had never had the burned out and destroyed properties as other areas. After a couple of years they returned to Denver where he took over the church.

"Papa, why did I have to come home? I was with Abe," Seth asked, as he grabbed hold of Jonah's pant leg and looked up at him. Jonah swung his baby up into his arms, placing him on his hip. "Because you're my little boy and at night I want my kids safely tucked in their own beds. Besides, Mama would be mad if her baby boy didn't come home."

"I'm not a baby. I'm almost as tall as Jacob."

"Well, you're getting there. It won't be long, but you don't want to get Mama mad do you?"

"Uh uh! Nope"

"I didn't think so!   Hannah! Joseph! Jacob! It's time. Get home now!"

"We're coming, Papa," yelled Hannah.

All three children scooted to a stop as they came up beside their father. Jonah herded them into the house. He set Seth down on the porch behind them. Sunny rose from the porch swing and smiled at her husband as he put his arms around her waist.

"That's the hardest job I have, getting those little rascals in at night."

"Wait until they're old enough to be gone at night. What then?" she said, smiling, as she circled her arms around him, looking into his face.

"Sit around like some old granny worrying about them every minute, I suppose." he said, looking at his still beautiful wife, smiling back.

"No Jonah, you're teaching your kids good things. You will be proud of them."

"I already am Sweetheart. They have their mother's sweet and gentle heart."

"And their father's strength and good sense so how can we go wrong?"

"We can't," he answered as he looked into his other half's face. Who would ever believe that the young girl he had first laid eyes on in St. Jo would have made his life complete. He had no doubt that God led her right into his life and into his arms. He didn't make it so easy that he would take everything for granted. No, never. Jonah never failed to thank God every day. He could lose anything but not his family. He walked into the house her grandfather had built for them, but the home Sunny had made, with his family all enclosed inside.

The End

11064019R00104

Made in the USA
San Bernardino, CA
06 May 2014